Shadows of Deception

Anne Valle

Barefoot Publications

ISBN: 979-8-9891850-0-9

Cover design by: Karen Putz

Printed in the United States of America

To my husband, who always believed
and encouraged me to write.

PROLOGUE

The Letter

Shannon stared at the envelope. The same familiar slant. The same crisp lettering. Everything was the same. The handwriting was just as she remembered.

She closed her eyes and thought back to high school.

Tony Ambrose.

Her heart skipped to a familiar beat, the same *thump-a-thump* she had long ago forgotten. She remembered the rough, calloused hands softened by hours in the pool. The deep blue eyes that sparkled with flecks of green. The grin that started at the corner of his mouth and lit up his whole face.

In many ways, Tony was her "it's complicated" friend in high school. They both shared a love of horses that few others in their lives understood. They bonded over rodeos and spent hours riding together. The two of them could talk for hours about a variety of topics, going deep into subjects that the average high school student wouldn't even touch.

More than twenty years had passed since Tony's last letter. Their written correspondence began as notes passed back and forth between classes in high school. Then came postcards sent from military bases around the world. The postcards were occasionally replaced by letters–pages and pages of stories, adventures, and deep thoughts.

The moment she told him of her love for another man, the letters stopped. Shannon and Tony drifted apart, each of them deep into their own lives.

More than twenty years.

She missed him. They were never lovers; their friendship ran deep, a rare closeness between opposite genders that transcended love. There was a passion between them that muddled the lines of their friendship more than once.

Her heart beat faster as she wondered what the letter was about. The years had gone by in a flash. It had been a long time since her heart raced at such a fast pace.

Opening her eyes, she glanced at the return address.

Texas State Penitentiary.

The High School Years

1.

"**H**ey, gorgeous!"

Shannon looked up and stared into the brightest pair of blue eyes she had ever seen. The strong smell of chlorine permeated the air, mixing in with hot, humid air that barely stirred.

"I'm Tony Ambrose."

He was tall and lanky, with the broad shoulders of a dedicated swimmer. One corner of his mouth broke into a lazy grin. "So, I see you're a newbie aiming for the girls' swim team?"

"I'm Shannon," she smiled. "I'm trying out. I've never really had a formal swim lesson, so this may be a challenge."

"You've never had a lesson? Well, let me give you some advice. All you have to do is charm Coach Parker and you'll make the team. Just flash him one of your pretty smiles and you'll win him over."

"I'd rather win on my talent in the water," she shot back.

The truth was, Shannon had no competitive swimming experience. Shannon's family purchased a tiny cottage when she was eleven and she spent her summers casually swimming in Silver Lake. Nearly every weekend, she and her sister piled into the family van and their father drove two and a half hours to their lake home. Shannon's best friend, Marie, often joined them.

Standing at the edge of the 25-meter pool, Shannon was feeling very much out of place.

"Oh, a feisty one, aren't we?" Tony flipped a lock of dark brown hair off his forehead and shot her a bigger grin. "I'll be keeping an eye on you." He sauntered over to the bleachers and joined a group of guys standing in a circle. Tony pulled his T-shirt off and slipped off his board shorts. Shannon's heart skipped a beat. She tried not to look at the skimpy scrap of navy blue nylon masquerading as a swimsuit. There wasn't much left to the imagination. The heat was rising in her cheeks. She turned and walked over to the girls gathered at the end of the pool.

"I see you met Tony," Marie said. "He's a senior. Watch out for him. He's a charmer. I think every girl in Northland High has the hots for him."

"Well, he's certainly attractive–I mean, have you seen his body? And there's something about that smile of his that just sucks you in." Out of the corner of her eye, she saw Tony dive off the starting block and break the surface with even strokes.

"Don't fall for him, girl!" Marie gave her a shove. "I heard he's a player. Rumor has it he's had just about every girl on the swim team. Oh, and the volleyball team, too."

Marie was Shannon's best friend. Their friendship began back in kindergarten when they met on the first day. During playtime, Marie walked over to a cabinet and came back with a pair of scissors. The two of them settled in a corner and passed the scissors back and forth, giving every doll a new look. By the end of playtime, Shannon and Marie had bonded. The teacher was not happy with the collection of dolls sporting newly-chopped hairstyles.

Over the years, the two of them styled each other's hair and spent hours at the mall trying on clothes. Shannon envied Marie's thick, black, shiny mane which needed little care to look good. Shannon's frizzy, auburn curls had a life of their own and she was forever trying to tame them into submission with a flat iron. Marie had skin that turned a golden brown in the summer sun. Shannon had to slather sunscreen over her freckles to keep them from multiplying.

Marie received a Nikon camera for her middle school graduation present and she spent hours taking pictures, prompting Shannon into different poses and dragging her to different spots around town. "I'm gonna be a photographer and go all over the world shooting covers for magazines," Marie announced one day. Shannon had no clue what she wanted to "be" as an adult.

"I'm kind of nervous about this tryout. I hope I don't look like an idiot out there," Shannon said. She pulled her hair into a ponytail.

"Just watch everyone else and do what they do," said

Marie. "You'll learn as you go. Do the butterfly just like I taught you and you'll do fine."

"I wish I had joined your swim team all these years. At least you know what you're doing."

"Alright, girls, gather around!" Coach Parker's voice echoed in the cavernous swim arena. "I want you to line up five deep at the starting blocks and give me 50 meters of freestyle. I'll be watching for speed, form, and execution. Then we're going to split up in teams and run some heats. And ladies, please ignore the guys–they've already had their tryouts and they're just doing drills today. I've already warned the guys to keep their eyes to themselves or they'll get extra laps."

Coach Parker had been coaching for 28 years. He was known for his monthly "Killer Saturdays"—four solid hours of distance swimming alternating with sprints of every stroke and only one ten-minute bathroom break. There was a rumor going around that the swimmers were taking potty breaks in the pool because they couldn't hold their bladders long enough for the single bathroom break.

By the second hour, Shannon was exhausted. She had never swam so many laps before. She climbed out of the pool and wrapped a towel around her. As tired as she was, she never felt more alive. There was something about the water which soothed her and brought her a calm feeling as she pushed through each stroke.

The girls gathered around the coach, waiting for his dismissal. "You all did a great job today," said Coach Parker. "We have another session tomorrow after school and the results will be posted Friday morning at the swim office. Now get going and hit the shower."

Marie and Shannon grabbed their bags and trudged toward the locker room. They were too tired to talk. Tony came running over. "Hey, you two beautiful babes!" He pointed at Shannon. "I was watching you in the pool and for a freshman, you have some serious potential. I can't believe you have no formal swim training. You swim like a fish!"

Shannon smiled. "Thank you. I hope I make the team. And hey, I thought the coach warned you guys to keep your eyes to yourself!"

"Well, the beauty over here was dazzling! It was like a giant beacon of light–kind of hard to ignore." He grinned at Shannon. "Remember, just turn the charm on Coach, and you'll be in." Shannon rolled her eyes at him.

"Notice how he didn't say a word to me," Marie said as they walked into the locker room. "Like I said, he's quite a charmer. I think he has the hots for you. Just steer clear of him–remember, he has a reputation."

Friday morning couldn't come soon enough. After they got off the bus, Shannon and Marie ran to the swim office and pored over the list.

"We both made the team!" Marie squealed. She grabbed Shannon in a hug and jumped up and down.

"I can't believe it!" said Shannon. "I'm so freaking excited!"

"Me too! Okay, we've gotta run to class. I'll see you at lunch."

"See you at lunch!"

Shannon turned the corner to head to her first class and she ran into Tony. Literally smack-dab into him. "Whoa, there, Red, what's your hurry? Judging from the smile on your face, I'm going to guess you made the team?"

"Yeah, I did!" She couldn't keep the grin off her face. She wasn't sure if it was from the excitement of making the team or the feel of Tony's hand on her arm.

"Well, I'll see you this afternoon at practice then. Watch where you're going. Don't go bowling over all the guys in school." He gave her arm a playful squeeze and took off for his class.

Every day, Tony started popping up everywhere she went. In the hallways; in the lunchroom; and at every swim practice. He was definitely a ladies' man as he could be seen flirting with every girl all over the school. Yet, every time Tony poured on the charm with her, Shannon's heart melted. One day, Tony grabbed her in the water during one Saturday morning swim practice and dunked her. She gasped in surprise and swallowed some water. Coughing, she reached the surface and she felt his hands on her waist, holding her above water.

"I'm sorry, did you swallow some water?"

"You rat!" She exclaimed. She splashed water in his face and then pushed him underwater. He popped back up, grinning from ear to ear. "Feisty, aren't we?" He dunked her again. Kicking furiously, she broke the surface and turned to look for him. He was grimacing.

"Oh, I hit the family jewels, didn't I? That'll teach you to mess with a girl," she laughed.

"That's some kick you have. You should have no problem breaking some swim records!"

Coach Parker's whistle pierced the air and everyone swam to the end of the pool. The next two hours, the teams took turns swimming lap after lap.

The next day, Shannon was running late to her third period class when she saw Tony coming down the hall. Without saying a word, he pressed a note into her hand and took off as the bell rang. Shannon ran to her class and slid in her seat. The teacher shot her a warning look.

Shannon waited until the teacher turned to the board and carefully unfolded the note. *A note from Tony!* Her heart was beating 200 beats a minute.

Hey Shannon! I'm bored in this History class so I figured I'd write you a note to pass the time. History and Math are not my favorite subjects so I usually doodle in those classes. I love Art, Philosophy, and English class. My favorite class last year was the woodworking class. I made my mom an outdoor table. How about you? What are your favorite classes? Least favorite?

I've been watching you in practice and I gotta tell you, you are really improving! You're starting to get the hang of the butterfly and if you keep working hard, you will be able to break some records. Just keep building up your stamina. The butterfly is the most demanding stroke and often the ones who have strength and a tough mindset are the ones who break records. You can do it. I'm not just saying this, I really mean it. Besides, you look damn good in that swimsuit.

Tony

Shannon glanced around the room. She didn't want anyone to see the ear-to-ear smile on her face. For one brief moment, she wished *she* was his girlfriend. There was only one problem; he already had a girlfriend. Lisa Steffins showed up at every swim meet and she was often anchored on Tony's arm. Lisa was a popular girl—her long, wavy blonde hair and perfectly-sculpted body had many guys wishing they had her on their arm.

Shannon scribbled a note back and passed it to Tony in the hallway at the end of sixth period. Before long, they had a routine going. Every morning, Shannon received a note. Every afternoon, she passed one to Tony. They began to open up to each other in their notes. There was something comfortable and familiar about the process of writing out their thoughts and sharing them with one another. Besides, the notes helped pass the time during their classes.

Hey Red, you're getting faster and faster on the water each week. I can already see the improvement. Your hard work is starting to pay off! You did great with the freestyle leg of that relay!

So, tell me about some of your hobbies. What do you do on the weekends when we don't have swim meets? I'm usually at my Uncle Tom's ranch which is about a half hour from here. I grew up riding horses and going to rodeos. I work for my uncle, mucking stalls and doing odd jobs around the ranch. Two years ago, I started competing in calf roping contests and I'm working my way up with my skills. Plus, I look pretty good in a cowboy hat and boots.

Tony

Shannon could hardly contain her excitement. She absolutely loved horses! Two years ago, Shannon took riding lessons at a local equestrian center. Her riding skills were just beginning to emerge by the end of the six-week course. The Sunday afternoon lessons were the highlight of her week. She wanted to continue with riding classes but her parents were going through financial struggles. The horseback riding lessons were one of the first things clipped from the budget.

Shannon quickly scribbled a note back to Tony.

Hi Tony,

I was absolutely thrilled to see you love horses and rodeos. Two years ago, I started riding lessons at the Marionville Equestrian Center. I took six weeks of lessons. I'm still a beginner, but I love horses and everything about riding. My dream is to someday live on a ranch and ride all day! I've never been to a rodeo but I'd like to see you compete sometime.

My parents just gave me some devastating news. They are selling the lake home. We have a place on Silver Lake. My dad's job is not doing well. I'm heartbroken, I love going to the lake on weekends and during the summer. I'm so freaking sad right now. We only have a few more weekends left as my dad thinks it will sell fast.

I'm so bummed out.

Shannon

Every day, the notes went back and forth. Little by little they discovered new things about each other. Some days, the notes were short. On other days, they filled two or three pages back-to-back. Occasionally teachers caught them writing in class and reprimanded them.

Hey Shannon,

Sorry I didn't get to see you at the swim meet over the weekend. Coach Parker said you were sick. Hope you're feeling better soon! The pool was lonely without you.

I was in the medley relay (swimming the fly) and we took first in that. I took second in the 100 fly and swam my first individual medley—I came in dead last. It was kinda embarrassing, but not every race goes the way you plan. My leg cramped up during the last couple of seconds and I just couldn't push through the pain well. Coach was not happy, he gave me a lecture about "manning up" during competition. Needless to say, I need more practice at longer distances so that I can sprint through the shorter ones.

Congrats on your third place in the freestyle. That's quite an accomplishment for a gal who first joined the team with no formal swim training! I'm sure Coach Parker was also charmed with your pretty smile (Sorry, just had to throw that one in)!

See you at the next practice!

Tony

Shannon wasn't sick; her family piled in the car and went up to the lake that weekend. It was the final weekend. The lake home had a new owner. Shannon took a few mementos from her room and packed them into a plastic bin. Cindy sat on her twin bed, bawling. Shannon started to cry. The white lace bedspreads and pink pillows were so much a part of their childhood.

In the kitchen, her mom was crying too. She wiped the tears from her face. "This place will bless the next family."

"I can't believe how much we're leaving behind."

"I know, Shannon. Just remember, we bought this place furnished and we're leaving it all for the next people to enjoy. I hope they get as much joy as we did out of this place."

Shannon and Cindy were quiet on the way home. A chapter of their childhood was now closed.

One afternoon, Tony stopped her in the hall. "Hey, why don't you come with me to my uncle's ranch this weekend after swim practice? You can work on your riding skills. I'll even teach you how to rope a calf."

"That would be awesome," Shannon said. "But what about Lisa? Will she mind if I go?"

"No, she won't–she doesn't share the same love of horses," he said. "I've gotta run to class, but I'll write you a note. See you at the pool later."

At the pool, Tony pressed a note into her hand. "Here you go, Red. Stick it in your backpack and you can read it after practice. Meanwhile, time to work on that butterfly of yours."

On the ride home, Shannon unfolded the note.

Hey Red,

I'm really excited about us riding together. My uncle's place is about 30 minutes away. Lisa doesn't like horses, unfortunately. She's actually allergic to them as well as dogs and cats. So she never goes with me to the ranch or to the rodeos. She almost never comes to my house because of my pets. Plus, my mom's not too crazy about her.

I'm so happy to find someone who shares the same love of horses. Even my own brother, Michael, has no interest in horses. I mostly ride with my uncle, but he's often busy. My aunt used to ride with me but she developed an autoimmune disease and her back hurts a lot. She stopped riding a few years ago. I have a few friends that I have met at rodeos, but no one near me who loves riding as much as I do. I'm really looking forward to showing you the ranch and watching how you ride.

We'll leave right after practice. Why don't you get a ride to school and I'll drive you home afterwards. This is going to be a lot of fun!

Tony

2.

Shannon was nervous when she met up with Tony after practice, but he quickly put her at ease with a couple of lame jokes. He sported an old pair of jeans with a blue plaid shirt thrown over a black tank top. "I've got a dusty, black cowboy hat in the car to complete this fashionable look," Tony laughed.

"Marie is the fashionista, not me," Shannon reminded him with a smile.

"In that case, you won't mind the dust on the hat."

When they arrived at the ranch, Tony's uncle Tom met them at the gate and Tony made the introductions.

"It's nice to meet you, Shannon," Tom said. "Tony has talked a lot about you and tells me you love riding. I took the liberty of saddling up two mares. I'm on my way out, but make yourself at home."

"Thanks for letting me have this opportunity," Shannon said. "It's not often I get to ride, so I really appreciate this."

Shannon and Tony made their way to the corral. The heat magnified the fragrance of "ranch perfume," a mixture of farm animals and manure that permeated the air, making it difficult to breathe. Shannon could feel trickles of sweat down the back of her shirt. Her curly hair was constrained in a long braid and her red cowboy hat provided some relief from the intense rays of the sun streaming down.

"Before we go riding, I'm going to teach you how to lasso. You have to pass a test first," Tony grinned.

"Hey, that's not fair, I've never handled a rope."

"Who said life was fair?"

The two of them spent thirty minutes going over the fine art of lassoing a post stump. It took Shannon countless tries before she finally snagged the post. Tony slapped her a high-five.

"That's it, girl! Once you do three in a row, we'll hop on the horses."

Shannon rolled her eyes and aimed at the stump once again.

Ten minutes later, Shannon triumphantly pulled the rope tight on the post for the third time and threw the other end at Tony. "Let's go riding!" she said. They walked over to the horses tethered to the fence post.

Tony grabbed the reins to a beautiful palomino and patted the saddle. "Here, this one is Sunshine. She's yours. Hop on." Shannon put her foot in the stirrup and swung herself up. The horse took a few steps back and Shannon steadied herself. Tony climbed on a chocolate brown quarter horse and trotted up to Shannon.

"Let's go, girl. Let me see how you ride. Put her through a trot, canter, and a gallop."

Shannon felt a wash of nervousness sweep over her. "Remember, I'm rusty," she said. "It'll take me a while to 'get back in the saddle,' so to speak." She grinned. She rode around the corral, putting the mare through the paces. She was out of breath when she pulled up to Tony.

"Girl, I can't believe what I'm seeing–you're a natural! It's like you're one with the horse," Tony said.

"Sunshine made it easy–she's well-trained and very forgiving!"

"She's a good mare to ride, that's for sure. Hey, you know what, let's hit a trail. I know a secret spot that's really nice. It's an awesome piece of nature. Come on, follow me." Shannon and Tony rode in comfortable silence, weaving through a thick forest on a narrow trail. Shannon pushed her hat back. It was a relief to be out of the hot Texas sun. In the distance, a woodpecker tapped out a rhythmic staccato on a tree.

"When is your next rodeo?" Shannon broke the silence.

"I'm doing the Texas Classic in two weeks. You want to come and watch?"

"I would love to. I've never been to a rodeo."

"It's a date, then. Well, not quite a date, but you know what I mean." He gave her a wink.

"Are you sure Lisa won't have a problem with me tagging along?" Shannon asked.

"Listen, Red, you and I are friends and I'm happy I get to share this part of my life with someone. Bring Marie if you want. Lisa couldn't care less about rodeos. She wants nothing to do with this part of my life. She's never even been on a horse. I can't even convince her to pet one because of her allergies."

They continued to ride in silence as the trail became narrow and rocky.

"Whoa."

Tony pulled back on the reins. Both horses stopped. Shannon heard the sound of water bubbling nearby.

"Take a look," Tony said. Shannon followed Tony's gaze and gasped. They were in the middle of a lush, green paradise. Bluebells dusted the banks along with clusters of daisies. A narrow creek cut a path through the trees with branches hanging over the banks.

"Wow, this is absolutely beautiful," Shannon said. "I can't believe how green everything is–it's like a hidden part of Texas. I would totally come here to get away from life!"

"I often do," Tony said. "Sometimes I come here just to think or to take a swim. I should have had you bring your suit. Or hey, we could jump in there now and do a little skinny dipping," he teased.

Shannon blushed. "I don't think so."

"I'm kidding, Red, I'm kidding. Get used to it. Let's just sit on the banks for a bit and take a break. Besides, I want to get to know what goes on in that head of yours."

Tony dismounted and tied both horses to a nearby tree. Shannon followed him to the edge of the creek and sat down.

"Have you ever brought Lisa here?" She asked.

"Unfortunately no," he said. "Like I explained before, she really has nothing to do with this hobby of mine. Besides, with her allergies, she isn't a fan of horses anyway. There's no other way to get here except by horseback. That's why I'm happy I get to spend time with someone who appreciates this part of my life. In a short time, you've become a great friend, Red. Now, come on, tell me, what are some of your dreams? What do you plan to do after high school?"

"I, uh, don't really know yet," she said. "Probably something in the health field, either ultrasound tech or maybe nursing. I'm the opposite of Marie. She wants to be a photographer and has very specific goals and dreams. I kind of dream of being a mom someday. What about you?"

"Well, college isn't my thing. I don't want to be stuck in some nine-to-five. I just want to fly planes. My dad took me up in a friend's home-built plane when I was four. I took some flying lessons when I got into high school and I know for sure I want some kind of career in aviation. I definitely don't want kids for a long, long time. I want to play and have fun, first!"

Tony leaned back on his elbows and gazed at the sky. "The only time I really feel free is when I'm on a horse or up there in a plane. I don't have a care in the world."

"Well, I'm not too crazy about flying," Shannon said. "I've

only been on a plane once in my life, and that's when my family flew to Colorado. Twice actually, if you count the flight back. I was terrified the whole time. All I could think of was the plane going down."

"I bet I could break you of that fear of flying if you come up in a plane with me."

"No, thanks. That's not a fear I want to deal with, especially not in a small plane. I like my feet on the ground, not in the air."

An impatient snort from Sunshine reminded them that it was getting late and time to head back. They rode quickly, reaching the corral just as the late afternoon sun began to descend in the sky. As they put away the saddles and cleaned up, Tony grabbed an apple from a pail. "Here, give Sunshine a treat and then we'll take off."

On the way back to the house, they talked nonstop. It wasn't just about swimming and rodeos, but deeper topics like politics and money.

"I want to work hard for like 25 years then retire and live off my interest," Tony said. "Money doesn't buy happiness, but it sure makes life a lot more comfortable. My mom's cousin is a millionaire and the most miserable guy I know."

"I disagree, money does buy happiness–look at my parents, they're out of money and have to sell the lake house. I was so happy there–now that happiness is gone. The lake house would still be ours if we had money."

Their discussions were heated at times, but they respected each other's views.

"Red, I really enjoyed my time with you," Tony said when he dropped her off at home. "I'd like to spend more time with you. If you want, I could train you in barrel racing."

"I'd like that."

"So, how was your date with Tony?"

"It wasn't a date, we just went riding together," Shannon reminded Marie. They were on their way to school on Monday morning. The rain beat a staccato on the roof of the bus, a much-needed break from the relentless sun.

"Listen, I heard from Katrina that Tony is just trying to add you to the notch on his belt. You better be careful, girl. I don't want to see you get hurt by him. He'll just toss you aside once he's done with you."

"Marie, would you knock it off? Katrina's nothing but a big gossip and she makes stuff up. Why are you even hanging around her? For the record, Tony was asking me just as a friend. In fact, we talked about everything–including his relationship with Lisa. He made it clear that Lisa is his girlfriend and we are nothing more than friends. Tony and I happen to like the same things–the kind of stuff that Lisa doesn't even have an interest in. So would you just relax? I'm not going to do anything I'll regret. Ever."

"Okay. Just had to warn you."

"Thanks, but I'm a big girl. I can take care of myself. Now, you wanna join me in some fun? I'm going to watch Tony in a rodeo next weekend. You know how much I love horses. You want to come with me?"

"Will he be riding shirtless?"

Shannon rolled her eyes.

Right after her first class, Shannon saw Tony coming down the hallway. "Hey Red, I've got something for you." He handed her a folded note. "Have fun in class." He took off for the gym.

Shannon slid into her seat in English class just as the bell rang. Waiting for the right moment, Shannon unfolded the note.

> *Red,*
>
> *I've been thinking about you all weekend. You are really special to me. I enjoyed our time together at the ranch and would love to ride with you again. I know we've only known each other a short time, but you've become a great friend. I can always talk to you about anything and you always stimulate my mind with those deep discussions of yours. I've never had a friend like you and I cherish our friendship. So when are you going to invite me to come to your house?*
>
> *I got detention this morning because I arrived late for the third time this month. It's just hard for me to wake up in the morning. I have to bike to school this week because my mom's car is in the shop.*
>
> *I heard you're taking the lifeguard class–I am too.*

Once I get my mom's car back, I can drive you to the class if you want to join me. That would save your parents a trip.

Gotta go, teacher's giving me the evil eye. See you in the pool.

Tony

A warm feeling enveloped Shannon. She cherished the friendship with Tony. In some ways, they connected on many different levels, unlike any friend she ever had. Even Marie would become impatient with Shannon when she brought up deep topics. With Tony, the deep topics were endless.

Shannon felt a thrill every time Tony passed a note to her. For just a moment, Shannon was jealous of Lisa. She wondered what it would be like to be the girl on Tony's arm.

Shannon took out a piece of paper and began to write.

Tony,

Thanks for the nice note. I really enjoyed our time together on the trail and I definitely would be happy to ride again. I talked to Marie, she is going to come with me to the rodeo. In fact, she is buying a brand new outfit because she says she has nothing proper to wear to a rodeo. She cracks me up.

We are watching a boring movie and I'm sitting way in the back so it's a bit hard to write this with

27

the film flickering. My English teacher is pretty wild. She's always wearing long skirts and has her hair in a bun. Kind of reminds me of the Laura Ingalls Wilder era. I don't know how she handles this Texas heat when she leaves the school. Who knows, maybe she changes in the Teacher's lounge. Ha.

If you want, you can come over to my house after school next week Tuesday. I have to study for a math test. Are you any good at math? I just suck at Algebra. I don't see why we need to learn this x + y stuff. You can meet my sister, Cindy as she is planning to stop by for dinner. She is older than me and in college a few hours from here. She and I get along pretty well despite the big gap of years between us.

I'll take you up on the ride to the lifeguard class. That class should come in handy. You never know when one of us is going to fall off a horse in the creek and need to be resuscitated.

See you in the pool.

Shannon

3.

Marie's father dropped the girls off at the arena. Shannon and Marie settled into their seats. They watched as a parade of flag girls signaled the beginning of the show.

"This rodeo isn't exactly what I expected," Marie said. "This place smells like animals and sweat." She wrinkled her nose in disgust.

"Well, I can't believe you bought an entire new outfit for a rodeo," Shannon retorted. "You look like you're doing a fashion shoot for a New York magazine. Those shiny black boots are a bit much."

Marie's mouth fell open. "What's the matter with having a little sparkle nowadays?"

"I think you're gonna blind the horses with all those rhinestones."

Marie shrugged and dipped a manicured hand into her popcorn. "Well, come on, already. When is Tony going to be doing his thing?"

"He's the second event."

The noise from the crowd was deafening. Rodeo fans were certainly a boisterous crowd. Shannon spied Tony across the arena. He was sitting on Goldie, a four-year-old quarter horse.

"Well, he's certainly a fine specimen, and I'm not talking about the horse," Marie said.

Shannon laughed.

"The next event is tie down roping," the announcer called. Tony was the first one in the ring.

Marie glanced at Shannon. Her eyes were mesmerized by the action. Tony was racing after a calf. He launched the rope and the calf stopped. Tony hopped off and ran to the calf, flipped the calf to the ground, tying three legs together. He got up, threw his hands in the air and hopped back on the horse. He waited six seconds to make sure the calf stayed tied. Tony tipped his hat to the stands. The crowd roared in appreciation.

"Shannon!"

"What?" She turned to look at Marie.

"I swear, you must be lost in love with the guy. Look at you. You're all flushed."

"I am not! I'm just fascinated with the whole process. Tony makes it look so easy. I can't help but feel sorry for the calf. And for crying out loud, it's hot in here!"

"Look, girl, I've never seen you so 'fascinated.' And

like I warned you since the first day of swim tryouts, Tony's a player. And right now, he's playing with Lisa and who knows who else. Rhonda from the volleyball team claims that she and Tony did it last Friday night after the game. I don't want to see you become the next notch on his belt."

"Marie, I swear, we are just friends. Besides, we both like horses. I don't know anyone else who likes horses like I do. I know it seems unusual for a guy and a girl to have a relationship that doesn't involve sex, but it can happen. That's what Tony and I have."

"Don't you ever think about kissing him? Or ripping his clothes off one night and having hot, sweaty sex? I mean, come on, look at that body! His muscles ripple in all the right places and that lazy grin of his is enough to melt any heart. Heck, I wouldn't mind taking a peek at that meat knot tucked in those chaps. I would make *him* a notch on *my* belt."

"Meat knot? Did you really just say that?" Shannon doubled over with laughter.

"Seriously, Shannon, don't tell me you haven't wondered about that. Or what it would be like to get in bed with him."

The heat rose in her cheeks. "We are just friends. I don't want to ruin what we have going on here. He's pretty open with what he shares about life and that's a rare thing coming from a guy. Besides, you're giving me mixed messages. On one hand, you tell me to stay away, and then in the next minute you have me in bed with him."

"Suit yourself, girl, but if you ask me, he's getting the best of both worlds by having you and Lisa in his life. Most guys don't have the luxury of having two girls at the same time. I'm surprised Lisa puts up with it, especially with the amount of time you two spend together."

Shannon sighed. The last thing she wanted to do was defend her friendship with Tony.

"Excuse me." The woman next to her stood up. Shannon was grateful for the diversion. She and Maria stood up to let her through.

As the rodeo went on, Marie grew impatient. The noise was too much for her and she could not wait to get out of there.

"Why don't we head downstairs now," Shannon suggested. The rodeo was about to end. "Tony should be out in a few minutes."

As soon as they reached the bottom of the stairs, Shannon spied a familiar cowboy hat among the crowd. She waved. Tony threw his hand up and weaved through the throng.

"Hey girl!" Tony enveloped her in a hug and grabbed Marie to pull her in. "Shannon tells me you aren't too fond of rodeos. I hope you enjoyed some of it."

"I managed," Marie said. "I've dragged Shannon to

fashion shows against her will so I guess it was payback time. But I don't think I'll be coming back."

"Well, thanks for watching."

"You were great," Shannon said. "Third place is not too shabby."

"Better than last," he grinned. "Shannon, you care to help me load the horse and equipment–I'll give you a ride back home." He looked at Marie. "That is, if you don't mind."

"No, go ahead, I'll be fine. My dad will be here soon."

Before she could say anything, Shannon watched Marie turn and head for the exit. Tony grabbed her elbow and guided her to the back of the arena. Tony's uncle was already loading Tony's horse into the trailer. "Just grab the saddles and the other stuff." Tom motioned to a pile of reins and ropes on the ground. A black box with a handle stood nearby. Shannon wondered why Tony asked for her help. His uncle had most of the equipment already packed up and the horses loaded.

"Thanks for the help." he slammed the truck lift closed. "I'll see you at the ranch tomorrow.

Shannon and Tony walked to the parking lot without talking. The silence was comfortable. Their friendship now felt like an old patchwork quilt. The conversation picked up once they settled into the car and joined the caravan of cars inching their way out.

"Hey, you know, it means a lot to me that you came out for this." Tony turned to look at Shannon.

"I really enjoyed watching you in the arena," Shannon smiled.

"I'm serious–not a lot of people would do this for me. Even my own mother doesn't come to the rodeos anymore."

"Don't get all swelled up in that head of yours. Remember, I like this horse stuff."

Tony laughed. He took his hat off and tossed it in the back seat. "Are you in a hurry to get home?"

"No, there's nothing else going on this weekend."

"You want to see the stars up close tonight? I've got a place where we can see the Milky Way for miles in every direction."

"Oh, another one of your 'secret' places?"

"Hey, you've enjoyed every single place I've taken you to!" He gave her a gentle shove.

"That's true," she smiled. "The stars better be spectacular tonight. I could be at home watching some great TV shows, you know."

"You'll love this, I promise you."

Twenty minutes later, Tony turned onto a rough dirt road. The loose gravel was illuminated by the full moon.

"Are you sure this is a good idea?" Shannon let out a nervous laugh. The headlights cut a path into the darkness.

"Red, trust me. This is the only place in town where you can see the entire Milky Way for miles around."

"The entire Milky Way?" She shot him a wry grin.

"Just wait."

The terrain became quite rocky and the truck began to strain as the road became steeper with each turn of the wheels. Tony steered into a grassy clearing and parked.

"Prepare to feast your eyes," he said.

Shannon stepped out of the truck and let out a gasp. In every direction she turned, diamonds glittered in the sky.

"What did I tell ya?" Tony grinned. He grabbed a blanket from the back seat and motioned to Shannon to follow him. They walked in silence to the edge of a cliff. Tony spread the blanket on the ground and they sat cross-legged, gazing at the sky. In the distance, a coyote howled. Shannon looked at Tony with a scared look.

"Don't worry, girl, nothing's gonna happen to you. I'll protect you." Tony scooted closer and put his arm around Shannon. She couldn't stop trembling. She wasn't sure if it was the strange howls or Tony's closeness that was sending vibrations through her.

She closed her eyes and leaned against him. The faint scent of sweat mixed with his musky cologne lingered in the air.

"You know...I've never brought anyone up here before. This is my secret spot. I come up here when I need to be alone and just think. So you're pretty special to me, because you're the first person I've brought up here."

Shannon looked at him in surprise. "You have never brought Lisa up here?"

"No, this was always my special place just to be alone. I come up here when life gets complicated–and it gets complicated a lot. With my parents going through a divorce, I just want to get away on most days."

"How long have they been married?"

"Almost eighteen years. My mom was pregnant with me when they got married. They've been fighting for most of it, so I suppose it's better that they aren't gonna be married anymore. My dad has a girlfriend. She works with him and she's way younger than him. What about your parents, how long have they been married?"

"Twenty six years. My parents are older. They were hoping for four kids, but they had Cindy and then couldn't get pregnant. They gave up on having kids after trying for a couple of years. I was a surprise baby. My parents didn't find out about me until my mom was about six months along. They have a good marriage, my dad treats my mom like a queen. He would do anything for her. That's the kind of marriage I want to have. They do fight, but they always seem to resolve things."

"You deserve that, Shannon. You're one of a kind. It's going to take a special guy to deserve a place in your life." He hugged her closer. They sat there in silence, gazing at the sky.

"Red–"

Shannon turned to look at Tony. He leaned over and softly kissed her. She pulled back in surprise and pushed him away.

"Tony!"

"I'm sorry. I just got caught up in the moment. I didn't mean for it to happen. It just felt natural."

"You've got Lisa."

"I know. I'm sorry."

"Is this why you brought me up here? So, I'm just another girl that you play with?"

"No–no, I really wanted to share the stars with you. I didn't mean it. The kiss, I mean."

Shannon stood up and walked toward the car.

"Shannon, wait!"

Tony grabbed the blanket and took off after her. "Come on, Shannon, I'm sorry."

"Just take me home."

4.

Shannon dreaded Monday morning. She contemplated taking a different route to her classes to avoid running into Tony. All weekend she ignored the messages from Tony on voice mail.

"Shannon, come on, give me a call," Tony pleaded. Shannon erased the message.

From the moment she arrived home Saturday night, her stomach was in knots. Did Tony like her more than as a friend? Was he planning on breaking up with Lisa so they could be together? Or was he just using her to get a few thrills and add to his ever-growing list of conquered girls? Maybe Marie was right after all. Maybe Tony just wanted one thing.

The phone rang and Marie's number popped up. "Hey," she answered. She knew Marie wouldn't understand the complexity of the situation and Shannon had no energy to explain her confusing thoughts.

"What did you guys do after I left?""

"Not much, we went for a drive and then he dropped

me off."

"That's it?"

"That's what friends do," Shannon reminded her.

"I thought maybe he took you somewhere and kissed you."

Shannon stared at the phone in disbelief. "How'd you know?

"What do you mean? He kissed you?!"

"Yeah."

"That complicates everything."

"Yeah, tell me about it. I haven't returned any of his calls. I'm sort of pissed. I thought I was more special than simply another name on his ever-growing list."

"No kidding. What are you going to do now?"

"I don't know. I'm a little confused by all of this. I don't want to be just another one of the girls on his list. You know he can be such a flirt. I like to think that our friendship goes way beyond that. I mean, I know more about his past, his dreams, and his struggles than even Lisa does."

"Did you kiss him back?"

"No!"

"Did you want to?"

Shannon hesitated. "Kind of. But that would really

ruin everything, wouldn't it? I mean, we've got a solid friendship–something really rare for a guy and a girl to have."

"Would you date him if he asked you?"

"I don't know. I mean...he's pretty solid with Lisa."

"Come on. You know you can tell me."

"I...I don't know. Really. It's all confusing. I gotta go..." Shannon hung up. The phone rang again and Shannon let it go to voicemail.

"Girl, get your head straight on this. Don't be another notch in his belt."

Shannon erased the message. She grabbed a glass of water and headed up to bed. The next morning, Shannon woke up at ten. She laid in bed thinking about the kiss. She closed her eyes and felt his soft lips upon hers.

What would have happened if she kissed him back?

With a sigh, Shannon grabbed a piece of paper and began to write.

Tony,

First of all, I enjoyed watching you at the rodeo. You did a great job. Even Marie seemed to enjoy herself, but she'll tell you otherwise.

Now, about what happened after the rodeo, I was just completely taken by surprise. I didn't expect that from you. I mean, you have a girlfriend.

And you have a reputation of being a playboy. I thought we had a pretty solid friendship going and your kiss threw everything off. I'm not sure why you kissed me. If you really loved Lisa, that would have never happened. You would be faithful to her.

I know it's easy for you to flirt with many girls. The thing is, I don't want to be just another girl on your long list. There are rumors out there that you're not even exclusive with Lisa.

I'm really not sure where our friendship stands at this point.

Shannon

On Monday morning, Shannon passed Tony in the hallway and silently gave him the note. He handed her one, too.

"Hey, Red..." Tony tried to grab her shoulder but she shrugged him off and kept walking. Halfway through English class, Shannon asked to be dismissed so she could go to the bathroom and read the note.

Red,

Hey there, how are you? I want to apologize for Saturday night. Ya see, I want to explain myself. I hope you never tell or show this to anyone. We've been friends for a while now and I've never had a friend like you. I'd be lying if I said I wasn't attracted to you or ever had the urge to tear your clothes off. I'm a guy, after all. Sometimes it's hard to control those urges. I didn't want to share that with you because it might hurt our friendship and I didn't want to lose that. Look what happened over a simple kiss. Ok, it wasn't simple to you, and I'm sorry. I would never, ever want to do anything to hurt you.

I don't want to lose you and your friendship. I think you know I wouldn't lie to you. I'm sorry I messed up. Can we have a do over? Whether you choose to believe my sincerity about our friendship is entirely up to you. I'm sorry. Think about it, ok? And please forgive me. I want our friendship to continue.

Tony

Right after lunch, Shannon ran into Tony.

"Have you forgiven me?" he asked.

She smiled at him. "Yeah. I don't want to lose our friendship, either."

Tony held his arms out. "Is it okay if I at least get a hug? I promise not to kiss you."

Shannon laughed. She couldn't help it. She wanted her buddy back. She gave him a quick hug. "Hey, I want to go riding this weekend. Can we saddle up at your uncle's ranch? I want to start riding barrels."

"Are you serious? Yeah, I would love to see you do that. Can you do Saturday morning at nine? It will be much cooler then."

They quickly settled back into their comfortable routine as friends. The energy between them was electrified when they spent time together, but they each respected the line drawn in their relationship. Their shared passion for horses was the bond that cemented them each and every time.

Shannon's skills were improving with each practice. When they weren't in the pool, they spent time together on the farm, racing barrels and riding the trails.

"Hey girl," I think you're ready to try your first rodeo soon."

"No, I don't feel ready for that. I'm still not leaning into each barrel."

"Sometimes you just gotta say 'yes' to opportunities and try them. I'm telling you, you've got a natural talent. You communicate with your horse very well—you just need to learn how to trust your horse for the turn. Come on, the next rodeo is a month from now. That's plenty more time for you to practice. Just say the word and I'll sign you up."

"I'll think about it."

Shannon's practice session went so well that her confidence increased. Maybe she could do a rodeo after all. Sunshine glided around each barrel with ease.

"Girl, you looked so smooth out there! Sunshine just loves you. She responds really well to you."

"You know what, I'm gonna do it. You're gonna have to help me get ready, but I'm game to circle some barrels."

"That's my girl!"

Shannon could feel the nerves shaking inside of her as she mounted Sunshine. "Remember, one to the right and two lefts," Tony said. "Sit deep in each turn and keep space around the barrel." The chatter from the crowd blended in with the announcer's voice. She stroked Sunshine's mane as she waited for the signal to start. Her first rodeo experience was about to begin.

Sunshine bolted straight for the first barrel and rounded it smoothly. They rounded the second barrel a bit wide and headed down toward the third. Sunshine turned tightly and was slow to get up to speed. Seconds later, it was over. Shannon pulled Sunshine to a stop with a triumphant grin on her face. She did it!

Even though she placed second to last in her division, Shannon was happy. Her dream of riding in a rodeo had come true.

"Red, I am so proud of you!" Tony hugged her.

"Thanks! I couldn't have done it without you. I know I

was a bit cautious and slow, but at least I stayed in the saddle and rounded them all."

"We'll work on speed next. It won't be long and you'll be racking up first place!"

On Monday morning, Lisa cornered Shannon in the hall. "Can we talk for a minute?"

Shannon nodded.

"Look, I know you're spending a lot of time with Tony. I don't mind you guys sharing your time over horses, but I want to make sure nothing's going on between you two."

"Lisa, we are just friends, nothing more."

"I am hearing rumors that you two slept together."

"Who is spreading that kind of rumor?"

"I have my sources, I'm not going to reveal them. I asked Tony if it was true, he said it wasn't. But, he's lied to me before. He's been with other girls throughout our relationship."

"Well, I can tell you the same thing, that's a made up rumor, nothing more. Tony and I have a friendship–we happen to like the same thing–and that's horses–"

"And swimming."

"That too."

"Well, you have a bond with him that I can never

have–I can't be around horses and I hate going in the water."

"Tony has always made it clear that you are his girlfriend."

"And I intend it to stay that way. So I just want to make this clear to you. Don't cross any boundaries with Tony or I'll make sure that you two never ride together again."

Shannon just nodded her head. There wasn't anything more she could say.

"I'll see you around." Lisa walked off.

The end of the school year came up fast. Shannon and Tony went to several rodeos together. Shannon's ability to barrel race improved tremendously. She had several ribbons hanging up on her bedroom wall. She never told Tony about Lisa's conversation in the hall. The less said, the better.

One evening after a rodeo, they drove back up to Tony's secret place to watch for shooting stars.

"I can't believe how fast this year has gone by," Tony said. "I really wish I was a junior so that I could have one more year hanging around you and doing rodeos together."

"It's going to be hard to say goodbye to you when you

take off for basic training."

"It won't be a goodbye, it will be 'until next time.' We will always be friends."

"Is Lisa in your future?"

"I think so, Red. I'm not 100% sure. Marriage isn't something I think about. Right now, all I want is to be in the sky and fly. I'm young, I have a whole future ahead of me, and who knows–maybe I'll meet a girl in every port." He winked. "What about you? I saw that you kissed Steve on one of our bus rides. It's nice to see you're not opposed to kissing! You two didn't last long."

"Steve is a great guy, but we just didn't hit it off. He's not a great conversationalist–we really struggle to find things to connect on. Plus he doesn't share my love of horses," Shannon laughed.

"There will be others, Red. You're a gem and some guy is going to be really lucky to be with you. I consider myself lucky as heck to have you as my friend and sharing my hobbies with you. I'm gonna really miss you when I go!"

"Me too, Tony."

They laid side by side in silence. Just then, a star dashed across the sky.

"Hey Red, will you sign my yearbook? Think of it as a permanent letter that I can look at for years and years to come." Tony smiled. "I expect a masterpiece." He handed her the yearbook. "Just give it back to me after science class."

"Sure. I left mine in the locker, but I'll give it to you this afternoon."

During lunch, Shannon sat in a back corner and opened the yearbook. It was hard to think of what to write. They had passed so many notes back and forth during the year. A wave of sadness enveloped her. High school would not be the same without Tony.

> *Tony,*
>
> *You made high school so incredibly special just by being my friend. Every day, I looked forward to getting a note from you and writing you one back. I'm actually quite sad that I will have to go through the rest of my high school years without a note to look forward to. I'm going to have to start paying attention to the teachers again. I hope you send me a postcard every week from wherever you are stationed!*
>
> *Thank you for your friendship and all that you've taught me in the horse world. You have literally helped me bring a dream to life and I've learned how*

to be comfortable in the saddle because of you. I love how you've challenged me during times when I didn't have confidence. It is through those challenges that I changed and grew. Thank you for that.

I could write pages and pages more and I know you were hoping for that, but I think you and I have said so much throughout the school year that it doesn't need to be written. It's already within us. Our friendship transcends anything that I've ever experienced in life and I'm grateful for that. I'm going to miss our conversations, our riding, and our time together.

I know that wherever you are, we will be looking up at the same sky, the same stars, and the same moon—and we'll be connected.

Hugs, Shannon

In the hallway, Tony and Shannon exchanged yearbooks. "I'll give you yours back tomorrow morning. I'll be crying all night writing it." Tony grinned.

"I didn't exactly write pages and pages," Shannon said. "I had to save room for all the other girls lining up to write."

"Very funny. See you tomorrow, Red!"

The next morning, Shannon opened her yearbook. Tony had written two pages in the back of the yearbook.

Red,

I sat a long time before picking up the pen to write. Where does one start when something is so special? Where does one start when a person has a unique, amazing place in the heart?

I've never met anyone like you Red. You are basically the yin to my yang when it comes to friendship. I will always cherish what we have together and the awesome experiences we went through this year. You made my senior year an incredible one. Up to now, I've never had anyone to share my love of horses with (well, except Uncle Tom–but he doesn't count!) so I treasure that part of our connection.

I have so many cherished memories to look back on. Like the time you kicked me in the pool–I'm pretty sure that one of my 'jewels' is permanently deflated. Just think, I bet no other guy gets to write about that kind of thing in a yearbook! The other things that stand out–I loved watching you progress in the pool. Those medals sure looked good on you! The first time you won a medal for the butterfly, I think I cheered so loud that everyone went temporarily deaf. Keep on working hard in the water and be sure to write and tell me about every meet in the next three years. I'll keep on being your biggest fan!

And in the ring—wow girl—watching you ride Sunshine is like watching poetry in motion. I swear, I saw a smile on Sunshine's face every time you walked into the stall to get her out. Red, YOU are sunshine in my life, too!

So, writing in this yearbook is bittersweet because I won't be able to write in the next three yearbooks of yours. Yet, I know this is just the beginning and we'll always be connected. Just think, we will have more adventures to write and share about in the upcoming years.

So Red, there's no goodbye here. Just a 'see you around!' You'll always have a place in my heart as a best friend.

Hugs,

Tony

There was a crowd of students at Tony's graduation party. He invited everyone from both the volleyball team and the swim team. The above ground pool looked like it was going to burst at the seams with so many bodies crammed together.

"Hey Red, can you stay a bit after everyone leaves?"

"Sure, I can help you clean up."

"Thanks, I appreciate it."

To Shannon's surprise, Lisa gave Tony a quick kiss and left early. As the last student left, Tony and Shannon gathered up the pop cans and plates.

"I can't believe you're leaving in two weeks."

"Yeah, the Marines waste no time in getting their recruits into action. I've got a long road ahead of me to become a pilot with them, but I'm looking forward to the learning that goes with it. Red, promise me that we'll always keep in touch. I'll send you the first letter when I get there."

"Yeah, I'm gonna miss writing you notes during English class and passing them to you in the hallways. High school isn't going to be the same without you."

"Come here, I've got something for you." Tony led her down the hallway to his bedroom. He handed her a small gift bag. "This is a little something to remember me by."

Shannon pulled out a small box. Tony had framed a picture of the two of them sitting on horses. Tony's uncle had captured the photo right after they came back from a sunset ride. The sun was bouncing off Shannon's hair and they were deep in conversation.

"We look pretty happy in this photo!" Shannon said. "I

remember that ride, we were talking about my second place finish at the Bremen meet."

"Yeah, Red, you finally learned how to swim properly in the pool!" Tony grinned. "Come here." He pulled Shannon close and rested his chin on her head. "I'm going to miss you so much. In the whole wide world, there's never been a better friend than you."

Part II

5.

Shannon's hands were shaking when she turned the envelope over to open it. It had been more than 20 years since she heard from Tony. After Tony left for the Marines, he became a pilot. The two of them kept in touch for four years, writing letters back and forth. Tony sent her postcards from various places around the world. Gradually, the letters became fewer and fewer. They each had gone on to their own lives at that point. Shannon was busy with nursing school and working two jobs. Here and there, a few men popped into her life but none of the relationships ever became serious until she met Gary. Once she told Tony about Gary, the letters gradually stopped.

In the last several years, Shannon occasionally searched the web to try and find Tony. She was a bit puzzled at the lack of information, until one day, she found a link to a small article detailing Tony's retirement from the Marines. He was honored for saving the life of a civilian in a house fire while home on leave. There were no social media accounts linked to him.

Tearing open the envelope, Shannon pulled out a Christmas card. On the front was a pair of hands holding a heart. On the inside was the inscription: *Those who are dear to us are always in our heart.*

Dear Red,

I know it must come as a bit of a shock for me to reach out after all these years, especially from a prison address. I asked my brother Mike to find your address so that I could write to you. I have a long story to share with you and I hope you can bear with me as I fill you in on what's happened since high school. So much has happened–some of it good, some of it great, and some of it terrible beyond belief. It will take me some time to tell you all of it. Meanwhile, tell me what you've been up to all these years. I hope you've been well and I can't wait to catch up with you. Wishing you a wonderful Christmas.

Tony

Shannon grabbed the phone and called Marie. She answered on the first ring.

"Girl, you are not going to believe what I'm about to tell you... I received a Christmas card from Tony."

"What? You've got to be kidding me! What's going on?"

"That's the thing, I'm not sure yet," Shannon said. "I received an email out of the blue from his brother Mike a week ago, telling me that Tony was in prison and that he was completely innocent of the crime he was accused of. That's all he would tell me, saying Tony would explain it all after he contacted me. He did say he was taking a theology class and reaching out to people who meant the most to him and I was one of them on his list. I didn't say anything to you because I wasn't sure what all this was about. Plus, you were in the Bahamas doing a shoot."

"I can't believe you didn't say anything. You two were close in high school, but my gosh, it's been years and years since you've connected. Why would he reach out now?"

"I don't know. I guess that's what I'll find out when I write to him."

"You're going to write to him? What about Gary? Is he going to be okay with that? I mean, come on, he knows you had a thing for Tony in high school. And you and Gary aren't exactly lovey-dovey right now."

"I know. I'll have to run this by him and see how he feels. And remember, nothing ever happened in high school except that kiss–and that was nothing. We were good friends. But, come on, Marie, it's not like anything is going to happen. The guy is in prison for crying out loud."

"Look, girl, don't go in too deep with this," Marie cautioned. "You're dealing with a guy who's doing time. He's probably reaching out because he's lonely or he wants something. Whether he's innocent or not, prison has a way of hardening a man and you don't know what you're dealing with."

"Relax, will you? I'm not going to jump off the deep end with this. I'm just going to respond and see what's up." Shannon changed the subject. "So, tell me about your Costa Rica trip."

Marie launched into her usual complaints of travel, the food, and the hot sun. She made it to the beach for a few hours and that was the best part of her trip. Marie was doing a travel shoot for a popular magazine. As much as Marie loved being behind the camera, she disliked the travel that came with her job.

"I gotta go," Marie said. "Let's meet up for coffee next week. I'm home next week." They agreed to meet on the following Monday.

Shannon glanced around the kitchen. The dishes were still in the sink, with the evidence of yesterday's supper still clinging to the plates. One of the boys left a carton of ice cream out all night. Shannon threw the soupy mess into the garbage. She spied a box of Christmas cards at the end of the counter and grabbed a card. She scribbled a quick paragraph to Tony, letting him know she was married and telling him a bit about the twins and her work as a nurse.

"Thanks for reaching out. I look forward to hearing more from you," Shannon wrote. She sealed the card, put a stamp on it, and placed it in the middle of the other completed cards.

Gary walked into the kitchen. "Is there any coffee left? he asked.

"You'll need to make some."

Gary let out a sigh. He needed a cup of coffee each morning before he could even begin to engage in conversation. Shannon knew it wasn't the right time to bring up Tony. She waited until Gary was halfway through his morning drink and she casually mentioned Tony's card.

"Why now?" Gary asked. "Where has he been all these years?"

"Well, he wrote from a prison," Shannon said. "His brother Mike swears he's innocent, and that he was framed. Mike didn't say what his crime was, so at this point, I don't know. I sent him a Christmas card from all of us. Hope you're okay with that."

"Hell, there ain't much he can do if he's behind bars," Gary said. "Don't be too sure he's innocent though. Nowadays, with the legal system, they usually catch the right guy."

"Well, innocent or not, we were close friends in high school. I'm just going to see what's going on."

Gary shrugged, got up, and put his empty cup in the sink. He slung a red tie around his neck, planning to knot it later. His work as a financial planner required a suit each day. "Gotta go." He grabbed his briefcase and a banana. Shannon watched as he disappeared through the door into the garage.

6.

A few days later, Shannon walked to the end of the driveway to get the mail. She instantly spied a thick letter with Tony's handwriting scrawled on the front and carefully opened the envelope.

Dear Red, Thanks for your card. That was one of my best Christmas gifts in a few years! Well, I've got so much to tell you that I'm afraid it's going to take a while, a lot of paper, and some tears. I'll tell you all, it's just not going to be easy, so bear with me. Thank you for being willing to re-establish our friendship. It means the world to me.

We've got so much to catch up on. While here in prison, I took a course called "Reinvention Path." Part of my homework was to contact people in my life who have meant the most to me. I gave Mike your name and asked him to locate you. He found you via Facebook as you and he share some childhood friends in common. I can't thank you enough for being willing to connect with me, given the situation. I know you didn't expect to find me in a Texas prison.

I'll start at the beginning of this journey I'm on. If you remember from my postcards, when I left home, I went for basic training at Camp Pendleton in California. I decided to enter the Marines because my father was a Marine. I became a pilot, mostly transporting soldiers and supplies. We moved from base to base until we were deployed in Desert Storm.

While I was home on leave, I met Denise through a friend while at a bar one night. Denise was on the dance floor having a great time and she looked like she didn't have a care in the world. I was attracted to that. She beckoned me on to the dance floor and I went. I had too much to drink that night. We fooled around and had some fun times together for a few weeks. Then I was back in the air delivering shipments of supplies overseas. Before long, I received a letter from Denise saying I had left a little "gift" behind and she was now pregnant with our daughter. I was a bit skeptical, as the baby was supposedly born early. The baby weighed 6 lbs 2 ounces. Denise sent me a picture of the baby. She named her Julie and insisted she was mine.

Several months later, I flew back to be tested and sure enough, the little one was mine. While I was home for two weeks, I slept with Denise. Stupidly enough, I got her pregnant again. We had another girl, Amanda (I delivered her, a story for another letter). Against the advice of everyone– my parents, my brother, and several friends– I went ahead and married her in a courthouse ceremony. I really wanted to be a good father to my kids and do the right thing.

After the war ended, I came home to a ready-made family. They were all complete strangers to me. Denise had an 8-year-old daughter, Taylor, from her first marriage. She had been divorced for six years when we met. I took a desk job as a recruiter and life settled into a routine. But at home, it was anything but routine. Denise was suffering from severe depression and she was diagnosed with bipolar syndrome. Life literally became a roller-coaster ride. I never knew when she would be suffering from the extreme mood swings. I found myself saddled with the kids during the times Denise had her "episodes." The shrink she was seeing just kept prescribing different medications, but nothing was really working. So Denise started self-medicating herself with alcohol. Her favorite was flavored vodka. I found empty bottles all over the house. Life became hell with her. We fought often. Denise worked as an administrative assistant and she stayed sober for her job, but in the evenings, I never knew what kind of situation I was walking into after work. It wasn't long until I despised being with her. Needless to say, you can't hide trouble in paradise from your kids.

They know when something is wrong, no matter how you try to cover it up. I always felt like I was walking on eggshells during my entire marriage. Some nights I slept on the couch in the basement just to have my own space away from her. Between her, the kids, and my job, I was stressed to the max and my stomach was in knots a lot of the time.

Even though my job gave me security and a steady paycheck, I really missed flying. I started looking for a job which would get me back into a plane– any plane. I was willing to take a Fed Ex job and I did. By this time, the kids were older and I began to bring up the idea of divorce. I was miserable in my marriage. The only time I felt good was in the air, on the job. I started filling in for other pilots every chance I could get. The money was nice, but I didn't care about it–I just enjoyed the life my job gave me. Once I came home, I devoted myself to the kids. Denise and I kept on constantly fighting, mostly about her drinking and all the pills she was popping.

Taylor was 15 when she started acting out and giving us trouble. She and I had always been very close–her biological father was never in her life. She began to blame me for her mother's troubles. At the same time, she started parading around the house in tight dresses. She was dating older guys, staying out all night, and disobeying our rules. I discovered she was no longer a virgin. Punishing Taylor never worked; Denise would always let her off. We were being played against each other and I didn't handle it well. Taylor and I got into an argument one day. By this time, she was almost 18 and ready to graduate.

I was on my way to work when I received a call from Denise telling me that Taylor packed a suitcase and left. She told Denise that I had asked her for sex and she was moving out to get away from me. I went home and found Denise high on pills and a bottle of vodka open on the counter. We ended up arguing at the top of the stairs and Denise stumbled and fell down. She was unconscious when she landed. I immediately called 911 and rushed her to the hospital. She was in a coma for several months. When she woke up, she told the doctors that I had touched her daughter. She also told the doctors that I pushed her down the stairs.

That's how my nightmare began. I was arrested and thrown in jail. The cops kicked me and beat me. For 16 months, I fought my case. Once a month in court, I was told what a jerk I was, calling me every name in the book. I was told over and over what a horrible person I was, even though there was no proof against me. I maintained my innocence throughout it all.

Just when it looked like all the charges would be thrown out, I was hit with some new ones. My wife accused me of hitting her and the kids during our marriage. I had never laid a hand on my wife or my kids. The one time I spanked Julia, I cried like a baby afterwards and vowed to never do it again. To be accused of such a thing was like a knife in my heart. I sank into a black depression so deep there was no light anywhere in my life. I didn't care if I lived or died. In fact, I felt like death would be a relief from the nightmare I was going through.

The final straw in this whole ordeal came when my lawyer advised me to take a plea agreement. According to him, all of the charges would be dropped except one. This meant seven years in jail vs. 60 years or more if I lost in trial with the original charges, especially with an attempted murder charge thrown in. I was told that my kids would be taken away and put in foster care if I attacked my wife's psychiatric history. There was no way I'd win a trial, my lawyer said. To top it off, Denise's father was the mayor of the town I was to be tried in. He had a lot of political connections. I knew he could make my life even more miserable with his powerful network.

By this point, I had run out of money. So in my darkest hour and greatest moment of weakness and fear, I signed the plea agreement and cast myself into hell. After 16 months of constantly being beaten in jail, all the accusations against me, the loss of everything—including my sanity—I gave in and really didn't care what happened to me anymore. I figured I was coming to prison to die anyway. And I did die–to my family, my friends, and my children. I became an outcast. Everything about my life before this ceased to exist. I never saw my kids again. My divorce became final and my family totally disappeared from my life.

When I arrived in this Texas prison, I didn't play nice with the other inmates at first. The Marines had spent a lot of money on me in the art of violence and I was not going to be intimidated by a bunch of "wannabe gangsters." I was a highly-decorated veteran who fought for his country–but in prison, I was absolutely nothing. It took a while for me to accept that I was lumped in with every criminal who landed there. I was now just a number in a prison uniform.

One day, I went down to the chapel, knelt at the altar and gave God what was left of my heart and my life. I vowed to be a student of His teachings. From that very moment, I was a changed man and things started getting better. I treated every person with respect and listened to them. My faith grew stronger day by day. I learned that being humbled and broken isn't a bad thing if it saves your soul. My journey is one of faith now and I have hope.

Obviously, Shannon, I've written the short version of what happened. I've got so much more to tell you. I hope I didn't overwhelm you and scare you off. I wouldn't believe it all if I didn't live it. So if you're skeptical, I understand. I hope you remember the guy I was in high school—that's still me. The one who loved horses, laughter, and fun. I just haven't been able to be "me" for a long time now.

Tell me about your life. Did you continue to swim after high school? What about riding? (I still remember our riding days with fondness.) I know we lost touch when you started dating Gary. Please tell him thank you for allowing you to connect with me. Catch me up. Tell me more about your kids.

I'll wrap it up here for now, but I am so glad you're back in my life.

Take care, Red!

Tony

Shannon let out a long sigh. What a crazy turn of events. For years, she had this feeling Tony would turn up in her life again. No wonder she couldn't find him on Facebook or other social media sites—he had been locked away in a federal prison for the last eight years. A prison! The idea of Tony as a prisoner was beyond anything she could have imagined. She walked into the kitchen, sat down, and read his letter again.

"So, what did your old flame have to say?" Gary's voice

pierced the silence.

Shannon looked at her husband. When they first met, she had told him about Tony and their friendship. Throughout the years, Gary had sometimes teased her about her "high school crush," after Shannon told him the story of the kiss.

Shannon and Gary met in college and after six short months of dating, she knew she wanted to marry him. Gary majored in finance and was president of the Investing Club. He was ambitious; dreaming of big homes and travel. Gary introduced her to spontaneous trips during spring breaks–last minute trips to exotic places she had never heard of. They kayaked on Antigua Island, saw monkeys in the wild in a remote town in Costa Rica, and stayed overnight at an ice castle in Canada.. Life with Gary was exciting and fun. Shortly after graduating, Shannon and Gary had a formal wedding with all the trimmings and 400 guests. They honeymooned in the Maldives, staying in a fancy hut on the water with room service.

Two years later, they had the twins, Zach and Brandon. Gary worked as a financial analyst for Cannion Mutual. He had no passion for his work, but the job enabled him to provide well for the family. They took elaborate vacations every year and they lived in a beautiful, sprawling ranch with a pool.

Life settled into a routine. Get up. Get the kids to school. Go to work. Repeat. Years later, Shannon and Gary were just going through the motions every day and everything in their schedule centered around the kids.

Shannon worked three days a week at St. James hospital as a labor and delivery nurse. She had long ago lost her passion for her profession and dragged herself out of bed on the days she had to work. The 12-hour shifts were very draining, but Shannon found it was better to suffer for three long days so she could enjoy her free time during the week. She enjoyed biking and working out. Twice a month, she volunteered at a local stable which ran a horse therapy program for children with disabilities.

"It's crazy, but Tony says he's innocent of the charges against him and he signed a plea agreement," Shannon explained. She shared the details from the letter with him.

"How can you be sure he's innocent, Shannon?" said Gary. "They don't just put people in jail unless they're pretty sure of the crime."

"That's just it. I can't be sure," she said. "But from what I'm reading and what I know of Tony from high school, he is sincere. I've never known him to lie to me."

"Well, don't get too wrapped up in this," he warned her. "The guy is in prison and that experience has probably hardened him. You need to be careful."

"Gary, you know me, I won't do anything crazy. It's just letters. Tony probably needs all the support he can get–prison is not a fun place."

"Well, I don't mind you writing to him, just don't get sucked into a sob story. Anyway, don't make dinner for me tonight, I'm going out with some of the guys from work for a few hours."

Shannon went into the living room and sat in the recliner with a stack of paper and a large book. she wasn't sure where to begin her letter. She thought back to the last time she saw Tony. He showed up unexpectedly at the door of her childhood home during her summer break from college. The long, soft locks from high school days were gone, replaced by the standard military cut. He was still handsome as ever, with the same lazy grin. Shannon was on her way to her summer job so their conversation was short. They quickly caught up on their lives and Shannon told him about Gary.

"Sounds like you've fallen in love," Tony smiled.

"I really have," she said. "I'm so sorry I can't talk longer, but I've got to run to work and then Gary and I are taking off to Cabo for the weekend. Maybe we can meet up the next time you're in town?"

"You betcha, Red. It's good to see you, however short. You look great and I'm really happy for you." Tony gave her a kiss on the cheek and a long hug. That was the last time she saw him. He sent her a few postcards from various ports around the world and then one day, the correspondence stopped. Shannon and Gary became engaged and Tony faded into her memories.

The cell phone jingled and Shannon snapped it up. It was Marie. Her voice had a tired edge to it.

"Yeah, the plane sat on the tarmac for two hours. I'm dead tired. It rained for three days straight in Portland. Everyone's hair looked like shit. One of the models was just getting over a case of shingles. I couldn't get any decent photos. Looks like I'll be doing a lot of photoshopping this round."

"At least you have a glamorous life snapping pictures of pretty people. Look at me, all I do is cook, clean, work, and chase after the boys. Gary's wrapped up in his own thing. He took off for dinner with some guys from work. We hardly ever talk anymore, and when we do, it's mostly about the boys."

"Hey girl, you know my life ain't all that glamorous. I deal with airport delays, lonely hotel rooms, and I'm shooting the same stuff over and over."

"Wanna trade?" Shannon jeered. She knew Marie's answer was going to be a wry no.

"Catching you up here, Tony wrote me a long letter and explained how he ended up in prison."

"What did he do?"

"Well, his wife fell down the stairs–quite drunk and with a lot of pills in her. She was in a coma for a while and when she woke up, she told the doctors that Tony pushed her. On top of this, his step-daughter accused him of suggesting that she sleep with him."

"That's warped. But it's probably true--I mean, they don't lock you in a prison unless there's proof."

"From what I understand, the cops basically beat a confession out of him. I've heard of that happening to people. There was no proof–it was her word against his–the same with the step-daughter. He took a plea agreement and he's about a year from parole."

"Well, like I've said before, don't get in too deep. Prison isn't a pretty place. He's probably hardened from being in there."

"I'm just writing to him, that's all."

"As long as it's nothing more–I'd hate to see you get wrapped up in this. You're married and you have kids. Well, girl, I'm gonna crash. I'm dead tired. Let's catch up more after I've had some sleep."

Shannon hung up and glanced at the clock. She had a half hour before she had to pick up the boys from school. She had three full days of work ahead of her so she knew she didn't have much time to write back.

Dear Tony,

Where do I even start? It's hard to believe that you ended up in prison for something you did not do. I know our justice system isn't always fair. My uncle Bob was framed for a crime he did not commit–he was accused of "cooking the books" at his company. My mom spent a lot of time trying to help his case. He passed away in prison when I was a young child. Later, they found out it was the secretary behind the money theft. She was having an affair with the owner and my uncle was the scapegoat in their affair. I can see how easily it is a case of their words against you.

So, catching up...I guess the most logical place would be to pick up the last time we saw each other when you came home on leave. I'm really sorry I brushed you off when you stopped by to see me. I was in a hurry to go to a work meeting and you caught me off guard that day. I had long ago moved on and our paths took such different turns after high school. If you remember from that visit, I was in nursing school at Washington University in St. Louis and that's where I met my husband Gary. Gary and I hit it off from the start, even though he was a financial guy and I was really into fashion at the time—quite a change from my high school days. I guess Marie finally rubbed off on me. I wanted to do something in the fashion industry, but I took the sensible route and got a nursing degree. As for Marie, she's living the life I kind of dreamed of—traveling to exotic places and shooting models in fashionable clothes. The funny thing is, she's really bored with her career. I guess the grass is always greener somewhere else.

I really can't complain because Gary and I have a nice life. We've been living in Austin since college, in a nice home in a great neighborhood. Three-

car garage, a pool, and lawn service. What more could a gal want? Well, besides a private chef and a maid!

Unfortunately, I rarely get around to swimming unless it's a few laps in the pool or a dip during a hot day. My days of leaping off the starting block are long gone.

Twice a month, I volunteer at a riding center doing therapeutic riding for kids. The kids have multiple disabilities. I really enjoy my time in the stables, even though I'm often cleaning out stalls or grooming horses.

Once in a great while, Gary and I take the kids to rodeos. My boys aren't interested in horses and Gary is allergic just like Lisa was– so they mostly humor me when I feel a need to hit a rodeo. Gary has to take a few allergy pills before we go. I did a few barrel races after high school but it was hard to find time to train and a horse to consistently train with.

The twins, Zach and Brandon, are now 16 and about to get their driver's license. Both boys play soccer and basketball. In the summer, they play on a traveling baseball team. Zach is my shy, reserved kid. He loves to game and plans to be a game designer. Brandon is the daring one and he's always outgoing and friendly. Brandon tells me he wants to be a lawyer–I just don't see him being the 9 to 5 type. The days fill up quickly with the kids' activities and school work.

Gary keeps himself busy with his investment club and regular golf outings. We've been married for 22 years. Sometime's that's hard for me to believe as I feel like high school was just yesterday.

I went into the basement and found the notes we wrote back in high school. I saved every note. Wow, what memories! Such a lifetime ago. No one else has ever shared my love for horses like you did. I was lucky to have you as a friend. You made high school so much fun!

Well, tell me more about your life. I'm sure the last several years have been very tough on you. I can't imagine what you're going through. I'll need to wrap this up here. I have a three day shift of twelve hours each coming up.

I have a crazy idea...could I stop in and visit you?

Hugs, Shannon

The next three days were long as Shannon dealt with one crisis after another at the hospital. She had little time for breaks as she ran from one patient to another. One mother gave birth in the hallway and Shannon caught the baby before the doctor arrived. In the evenings, Shannon went to the twins' games. By the time her head hit the pillow, she was beyond exhausted.

Two weeks later, Shannon received another letter

from Tony.

Red,

I'm so happy to be connecting with you again. Just being able to write to you makes the days fly by much faster than I've ever experienced. Seems like I've got so much to tell you and I am cautious about giving you too much information at once and overwhelming you. The nightmare my life has become is not uncommon. You saw what happened to your uncle–it's more common than people realize. I live surrounded by guys with stories even more bizarre and unbelievable than mine. It is the nature of this place. The thing is, what can I do about it? The only thing I can really control is how I choose to respond to what goes on here. Every day, the choice is up to me.

For a long time, I didn't care. I'd already given up. My only brother kind of disappeared for five years. He basically abandoned me after this ordeal happened. He was ashamed to tell anyone that he had a brother in prison–especially for the crimes I was accused of. My letters to him went unanswered for years.

It wasn't until he found God, in his own way, that he reached out to me. I cried buckets when I received his first letter.

In the last year, he's been back in my life and he believes in my innocence. He's the only one who has my back in the outside world. He knew in his heart that I didn't do the things I was accused of. I am humbled by his renewed faith and love for me. When he came back into my life, I decided I wasn't going to let this situation beat me.

I have written my kids lots of letters, sent them cards, and sent them messages through my brother, but I have not heard from them nor seen them since I've been locked up. Denise has cut them out of my life. My kids are older now; they've just gotta decide on their own if I still matter to them. Only time will tell, and I just have to be patient. It is the hardest thing I've ever been faced with—not being there for my kids. Prison is easy compared to that. I pray every day for another chance with them. They know I did not hurt them, except with my absence. I hope that one day they may remember their love for me.

Yes, you and I passed a forest of notes to each other in high school. Your notes always made my day. I looked forward to them each day. I don't think I learned anything during my senior year because I spent my class time writing you a note!

I have missed you! You were the friend who really understood me. I look back fondly of our riding times together. I gotta thank your husband once again for letting me connect with you as a friend. He must be a great guy to tolerate you writing letters to a guy in prison.

In the last letter, I told you about delivering my youngest daughter, Amanda. On the night Denise went into labor, we checked in with the doctor at the hospital and she told us that it was still too early to come in. Two hours later, everything was the same. We were in bed, watching a movie. Denise wasn't in much pain and the contractions seemed mild. Then all of a sudden, she started thrashing and yelling. I pulled back the sheet and saw my daughter's head. I wanted to reach for the phone to call the paramedics, but Denise gave a big push and I instinctively reached for my daughter. I caught her head and then the rest of her body slithered out. It was such a cool moment to hold my baby in my arms. I had missed my first daughter's birth, so this was all new to me. The placenta came out quickly. I went into the kitchen to grab a pair of scissors to cut the cord. I found some clean string to tie off the cord. We finally called the doctor and went into the hospital to get checked out. After a few hours, they sent us back home. Apparently we did everything right!

Amanda was so tiny. I was thunderstruck. All I could do was stare into those big blue eyes. She was an easy baby. Every day after that, she was wrapped around my finger. She was Daddy's girl all the way. Just writing this makes me miss my kids so very much.

To pass the time here, I play volleyball and

softball. In my early days as a Marine, I spent my free time on the court as a setter. The curse of a setter is to very rarely get a good ball to hit at. So all I did was clean up bad pass after bad pass and swing at junk. Sometimes the games become rough here and the guys start fights. You get all kinds of people in prison. My buddy, Joshua, plays on every team with me and we've got each other's back. You can't survive here without having someone to cover for you. The place is so noisy all the time. Sometimes it's hard to even think. Every single day, a fight usually breaks out somewhere. I steer clear of the troublemakers because they only make life miserable.

So what about you? What do you do for fun? Tell me about your nursing job. What's the best part about being a nurse? Do you have any "war stories" on the job?

I must admit, there are some days I kick myself for not staying in touch with you–after all, we were pretty close friends. I regret letting our friendship slide. I could always open up with you and we used to talk for hours. You are a rare gem, Red. I'm glad you're back in my life now.

Yes, you could visit me–I would have to submit some paperwork and get approval. Are you sure Gary would be okay with it? This is not a pretty place here.

Well, I want to get this in the mail, so you take

care. Thanks for your letter. Hope to hear from you soon. Tell the hubby "thanks" and hi from me.

Hugs, Tony

7.

On Friday night, Shannon and Marie went out to dinner at Viaccaino's, a new trendy restaurant serving vegan dishes. Marie had just wrapped up a shoot for Vogue and she was home again for a few days.

"I think I'm going to try the eggplant lasagna," Marie said. "Do you want to split that and get a salad?"

"Sure. But I want the chocolate cake for dessert. It's been that kind of week. Gary and I got into a big fight last night. He left and didn't come home yet. I'm guessing he slept on the couch at work."

"What was the fight about this time?"

"Gary wants to get another new car. It seems like we are on a revolving payment system. We never pay off our cars. This time, he wants a BMW. I don't want to keep shelling out money for stuff."

"What's wrong with the Lexus he's driving?"

"You know Gary, he likes showing off for his clients. He says it helps them to invest with him if they think he's super successful. Never mind that the car payments take a big chunk out of our paychecks."

"You could just quit your job and then Gary won't be able to swing car payments."

"No, he makes way too much money–my salary goes for fun extras, like my awesome set of nails here." Shannon waved her hand. She was sporting blue nails that looked like waves of water. "As much as I complain about my job, I like getting my own paycheck. Besides, it gets me out of the house."

"So how's Gary handling the idea of Tony being back in your life?"

"It's not really an issue, he doesn't seem bothered by it. I'm pretty up front and straightforward with him. I'm not hiding anything."

"Well, it does bother me a bit that Tony might be just using you, so please be careful."

"Look, we're fine. It's just a few letters back and forth." Shannon speared the tomato in her salad. "We were great friends in high school, but you know those days are over and I'm married. I'm not going to do anything stupid."

"Well, you and Gary are going through some rough times lately and this could be a tempting distraction. I'm just telling you to be careful, that's all."

"Look, I get it, I get it. For once, I'm enjoying a walk down memory lane and nothing more. It's nothing more than that."

For the rest of the evening, Shannon and Marie avoided the topic of Tony.

Shannon and Tony settled into a rhythm of writing back and forth week after week. She regaled him with stories of exciting births and the twins' accomplishments in sports. Week by week, Tony filled her in on his prison journey.

Dear Red,

Wow, thanks so much for your letter. I was sitting on my bunk studying my Biblical Hebrew course when your letter arrived. I can't tell you how much your letters mean to me.

It's too bad you didn't keep swimming after high school. You had so much raw talent. Besides looking damn good in a swimsuit, your butterfly stroke was a beautiful thing to watch! I was your biggest fan and I had a running bet with the guys that it would not be long before you were breaking records. I hope you've stayed in shape so you and I can race when I get out. The 50 yard butterfly–do you think you can take on an old man? I'll take it easy on you.

I really enjoyed getting to know your boys through your letter. It must be tough having the twins learn to drive at the same time. One teen with a driver's permit is bad enough–and you are going through it with two boys at the same time.

I taught Taylor how to drive and I'll never forget that experience. Denise wouldn't teach her (she couldn't function half of the time with the alcohol and pills in her system) so that was probably a good thing. Taylor was a very voracious, eager learner because she knew that driving equaled freedom and independence. I took her to the mall after hours and let her practice in the empty parking lot. I wanted to build up her confidence before she went out on the roads. I ran her through every drill that my uncle ran me through when I was a teen. Taylor had a few mishaps when she received her permit, but overall, I was proud of her. Spending that time together drew me closer to her.

One day, Taylor drove my truck through the garage door. She had just finished navigating an incredibly rough rush hour after practicing on the highway. She was feeling quite triumphant and was in a good mood. In her excitement, she forgot to put the truck in "park" and it was still running when she began to get out. The truck began to move, and in her haste, she hit the gas instead of the brakes. Wham! The truck rammed into the garage door, which was still closed. Talk about stunned silence. Taylor burst into tears. The new garage door cost me $1200. But it all worked out–

Taylor got her license and I bought her a used car. Before I handed her the keys, I explained that if she ever saw the blue lights in her rear view mirror because of speeding, she would lose those keys. Game over. You should do the same with your boys. It's an incredible motivator for safe driving.

Remember my best buddy, Steve? Oh wait, I know you remember him—you locked braces with him once after a swim meet. He told me he liked you back in high school. I know you dated him for a short time—I can't remember why it didn't work out? I don't know if you've heard the news, but he was diagnosed with stage-four brain cancer a few months ago. He hasn't been given much time. He's married and has five kids. He worked as a fireman until this hit.

Before he became sick, he sent me a letter. I only got one letter from him, but it was enough. He told me that he loved me and that's all that mattered. It took him a long time to come to terms with my prison sentence, but he decided to reach out to me despite the years that passed between us. I wrote him back and told him to get his heart right with God and I would see him again someday. Every morning when I hit my knees, I ask God to heal him if it's in his will. I've not heard any updates lately on his condition and he doesn't return any mail, so I can only hope for the best. I really don't want to lose him.

Well, say hello to the hubby and the boys. Take care. Hugs, Tony

Steve, ah yes, Shannon remembered Steve. He was a diver on the swim team. The kiss happened out of the blue. They ended up in the same seat on the bus after a swim meet and after a bit of small talk, Steve leaned over and kissed her. Shannon returned the kiss impulsively. They dated for a short time, but the conversation between them was often stilted and short. There wasn't much else to sustain a relationship and it quickly fizzled.

Ah, the silly stuff in high school. Shannon sat on the edge of her bed and shook her head at the memory. She looked at the empty suitcase on the floor. The four of them were leaving in the morning on an early flight to Colorado for a week of skiing and she wasn't even packed. Shannon pulled some sweatshirts out of a drawer and tossed them in the suitcase.

"Mom! I can't find my snow pants," Zach walked in. "Brandon found his pants in the bin downstairs but mine wasn't in there. Do you have any idea where they are?"

"Check the downstairs closet," said Shannon. "Your dad might have hung them up there with the ski coats."

"Okay." He bounded off.

The twins learned to ski on the bunny hills of Winter Park when they were three. They switched to snowboards when they were ten. Shannon and Gary preferred to stick with skis. Every year, the four of them headed out to the slopes in the west. This year, they were going to Breckenridge and staying at a hotel at the base. Shannon usually skied in the morning and spent the afternoons on her own. She was looking forward to curling up with a good book and some hot chocolate.

"Hey, have you seen my ski gloves?" Gary asked.

"Good grief, why is everyone asking me where everything is?" Shannon grumbled. "I can't keep track of all your stuff--I haven't even packed yet!"

"Sheesh, chill, woman! I thought maybe you would know where our ski stuff is--after all, you did a major cleaning of the closets last year and everything was moved around."

"Check the bin in the downstairs closet." Shannon walked in her closet and began to snatch sweaters from the drawer. She was tired and her hormones were rearing their ugly head. Her heart wasn't into the prospect of vacation this year. She didn't like the cold and dreaded the thought of shivering on the chairlift.

At 5 a.m. the shrill ringing of the alarm jolted her out of sleep. Gary reached out and slammed on the snooze button. "No time for sleeping in, we've got a taxi coming in 30 minutes," Shannon snapped. She roused the twins and the four of them quickly got ready.

The snow was falling in large flakes when the plane touched down on the runway. By the time they loaded the rental car and put the skis on top, everyone was on a short fuse. As soon as they hit the snow-covered highway, the boys went to sleep.

Shannon pulled out a copy of Danielle Steel's latest book and kicked off her boots. She was in no mood to talk and she was grateful for the fictional distraction.

Gary had other ideas. He was bored with the drive. "It looks like I'll be getting a large bonus next month. I'm going to put half in the 401K and the other half in the bank. I'm thinking of getting a new bike."

"Another bike? What's wrong with the Trek you have in the garage?"

"I'm thinking of doing the Leadville 100 next summer. I need to train on a different kind of bike."

Shannon looked at him in surprise. "That's a pretty tough race for someone who hasn't done a whole lot of riding. Where did this idea come from?

"We've got a new person at work who has done this before. She's done this three times."

"She?"

"Her name is Donna. In fact, she used to live near Littleton. She joined our team about two months ago."

"How come you never mentioned her before?"

"Just didn't think of it. It's not like you're interested in what goes on at work."

"Well, I just find it surprising that you didn't say anything. It's not often you get women on your team. It's mostly guys at the office."

"It's not a big deal."

Shannon shrugged and went back to the book. They rode mostly in silence until they pulled up at the entrance of the ski resort.

The next morning, Shannon went down to the gift shop to buy a postcard. She fired off a quick note to Tony. She added a stamp and dropped it off at the front desk.

The rest of the week passed slowly for Shannon. She felt a coldness from Gary that she had never felt before. He was distanced and aloof when they were alone at night. When they weren't skiing, Gary was buried deep into his phone.

"I thought we were supposed to be on vacation," Shannon snapped. "You've been on the phone practically non-stop since we arrived."

"Well, there are a couple of situations at work where I just have to respond to them."

"You didn't do that on our last trip."

"Remember, I was just promoted. I've got more responsibilities now."

Gary was mostly silent on the plane ride home and the boys slept. Shannon couldn't help but think about the great divide between her and Gary. She tried to imagine what it would be like once the boys went off to college. What would hold them together at that point?

Shannon was grateful to get back to work. The births were happening in clusters and she found herself running from one room to the next. The most exciting birth that week was a mom who gave birth to triplets-- she never made it to the planned cesarean surgery. Shannon caught two of the babies before the doctor walked in.

The postal carrier pulled up to the mailbox just as Shannon walked outside to get the mail. She smiled as she saw the familiar handwriting scrawled on the envelope.

Hey Red, I hope this finds you well. Thank you for the post card. I've been to Colorado a few times but believe it or not, I've never skied. I've mostly done the scenic stuff-- the Garden of the Gods and Pikes Peak. Before I got trapped with Denise, I stayed in Boulder with some friends and we often did some light hiking. On my last visit there, I was just learning the basics of rock climbing. We camped out in the mountains and I loved every minute of that trip. There's something about the stars there that reminds me of the night we saw the entire Milky Way on the top of that cliff. Do you remember that night? I tried to kiss you and you about slapped me silly.

Ever since I got married, I haven't seen my Colorado buddies and now they want nothing to do with me in prison. I wrote to them when this nightmare began, but I never heard from them. They basically shunned me after the news hit them. They still talk to Mike, but they want nothing to do with me. It hurts, but what can I do?

Well, guess what? Along with your postcard, I received your visitation approval confirmation. I am just simply amazed you are willing to come here and see me in this situation. Do you know there are those who've professed their love for me, friends who are M.I.A, guys whose lives I've saved at war and those who've saved mine--all of them would not do what you have done for me.

In Psalm 8:4, King David asks God, "What is man that you are mindful of him" and I've gotta ask you, who am I that you are mindful of me? I am humbled you would send me a postcard from your vacation. I'm humbled you would want to visit me in this hell. Whether you ever do or not, it doesn't matter. What matters is you were willing to do so. It is the thought that counts. You've already done more for my heart than most everyone else, including my own brother. He doubted me and he had to work through those doubts.

You are the answer to my prayers and you can

bet when I do see you, whether in here or when I get out, I'll be looking for a halo and checking for wings on your back. You are a true angel and I am so blessed to have you in my life now. I have become a pariah to everyone in my prior life because of this, so I can't thank you enough for your kindness. You really don't know what it means to me. Family is more than blood-bound—thank you for becoming a part of my family. It means the world to me. Give my best to your husband. I look forward to becoming his friend.

Hugs, Tony

Shannon couldn't imagine the pain Tony was going through--to be shunned by his own brother and his friends. She thought back to high school and remembered how close Tony and Mike were. They did almost everything together. From sports, to parties, to double-dates, the two of them were cut from the same cloth. The only thing they didn't share was a love for horses. Mike rarely attended Tony's rodeo events in high school.

Shannon did a search for Mike's number and located him in Indiana. She reached for the phone and dialed. There was no answer so she left a voice message. "Hi Mike! This is Shannon, a blast from the past! I've recently connected with Tony, thanks to your help, and I wanted to touch base with you on a few things. Give me a call back when you can."

Shannon closed her eyes and tried to imagine Tony in prison. Every now and then, a little niggling of doubt creeped into her mind. She heard stories of women falling prey to cunning prisoners who played with the hearts of lonely women.

What if Tony wasn't innocent after all?

This is different, Shannon reminded herself. *We were friends in high school and I know him pretty well. Besides, he's found a path back to God. Guys who have faith in God won't lie...*

Shannon put aside her doubts and sat down to write Tony back. Life settled back into a routine and Shannon eagerly waited for the mail each week. Gary was working later and later every night.

"What's going on at work?" Shannon confronted him one night. "Most nights the boys and I are eating without you lately. You've been missing their games. Is work really that demanding?"

"Look, I'm trying to work my way up to the next level."

"How much money do we really need? We've got a beautiful house, nice cars, and we go on lavish vacations. The boys have college funds. We've got money socked away for retirement. When is enough going to be enough?"

"Why are you trying to get in the way of my career? I don't get in the way of yours. If you wanted to work your way up to Director of Nursing, I'd be supporting you all the way. Why are you standing in the way of my career?"

"I'm not trying to stop you. I'm just saying we are drifting so far apart in our marriage. Your job is becoming like a mistress–I can't compete with that if you're constantly choosing the job over us."

"I just need you to stand by me for a while so I can work my way up. I've got big goals this year. It's just gonna require some sacrifice for all of us while I'm on this track."

"Well, before you know it, the boys will be in college and you'll have all the time you need at that point. I'm just saying that you need to be cutting back at work and having a balance with your family. If you don't, we may not have any family left."

"Dammit, Shannon, stop pulling this guilt stuff on me. I do the best I can for our family and I don't need you telling me how to run my life." Gary pushed back his chair. "I'm going out for a drive to clear my head."

It was 3 a.m. before Gary returned.

8.

The next day, the phone rang and Shannon recognized Mike's name.

"Hi there, Mike!"

"It's been quite a while, Shannon. How's everything?"

"Pretty good here. I can't believe how quickly the years have gone by. I know we aren't connecting under the best circumstances considering where Tony is. That's kind of why I'm calling you. I guess I just wanted to reach out..."

"Yeah, it's not the best circumstances, that's for sure. I couldn't talk about it to anyone for the longest time. Even now, it's still awkward. I mean, I can't exactly work my incarcerated brother into party conversations."

"Yeah, I haven't exactly told many people, just those close to me."

"Your husband is okay with it?"

"Yeah, I mean, Tony and I are just friends. We've

always been just that."

"Yeah, I kinda thought you two would end up together. You have a lot in common, especially with horses. You two were sure crazy about horses in high school. Do you still ride?"

"Yeah, every now and then. I volunteer at a stable for kids with disabilities and I'll saddle up once in a while."

"You're a good gal, Shannon. Not many people will do what you're doing, especially connecting with my brother again."

"Well, I know it hasn't been easy for him in prison. This is a little awkward, but I gotta ask... Tony explained that you doubted him at first and didn't visit for a long time. I wanted to ask you about that. I mean, one of my friends thinks that he's um, guilty, and that Tony might not be innocent. So of course, every now and then, I wonder about that."

"I get it. For a long time, I didn't believe him. I mean, it was his story against the story of a wife and teenager. And honestly, if you remember Tony's reputation in high school, he sure enjoyed the ladies up close and personal. So I didn't know what to believe. I didn't know what the truth was. Eventually, I just came to the conclusion that life was too damn short for me not to have my brother in it and I chose to believe him."

"Thank you for sharing that. That makes me feel better. It's hard to explain to others why I'm visiting a guy in prison, ya know?"

"Yeah, Shannon, I totally get it. Prison is definitely a dark place and it's hard for me to deal with the idea that Tony is in there with a bunch of crooks and murderers. But it is what it is and I deal with it. I know that when he gets out, he's gonna need support and I'll just be there for that."

"Thank you, Mike. Yeah, I plan to just continue being his friend. Well thanks for the call and catching up–you kinda helped me erase the apprehension I was feeling."

"Anytime. I'm sure our paths will cross again."

Shannon wrote to Tony, telling him how she connected with Mike and just caught up. She didn't tell him about the doubts she was having. She shared an update about the boys and Gary's career pursuit–keeping most of it light and chatty. She asked him about his parents–were they still around? She remembered Tony's mother–she was a kind, soft-hearted woman who worked at a bank. She had never met Tony's father. He was almost never around and Tony wasn't close to him.

Shannon thought back to the kiss in high school. Her initial reaction to the unexpected kiss was to push Tony away. She didn't want to be another "notch" in his belt. Tony had a reputation of sleeping around and the kiss only reminded her of that.

But the truth was, the kiss fueled a fire that was simmering inside of her. Every once in a while, she imagined something more. The attraction was real, but the friendship was so deep that she couldn't imagine ruining it with a romp in the bed. She ignored Tony's reference to the kiss. It was best not to go down that road.

Hi Red, thank you for your latest letter. I guess I should open with the bad news. Steve passed away. Mike called to tell me the news. My heart is breaking right now for his wife and kids. The Bible is right; tomorrow is not promised. There's nothing like a loved one's passing or a prison sentence to put it all in perspective. Live your life, Red. Every minute is precious because you can't get the moments back.

Well, now I'm in a "transition camp," a new program to prepare inmates for their release. It's a "short timer's" prison. Everyone here has two years or less to go. I'm not sure this is a good thing. The "time" here is harder and there's the potential for some serious violence as well as theft. There's a lot of aggressive guys here too and I have to deal with them. But it will be ok for the remainder of the time I have left. Not to worry, though. I promised my brother I would hang up my wrestling tights and keep my head down until this is over. Joshua didn't move with me, but I sure wish he would have. He's got a ways to go on his journey. Once we both get out, I know I'll see him again. He's like a brother to me and he defended me each and every time I was in a corner with these thugs here. I won't forget that. I've gotta look for a new volleyball partner here. I think I'll spend most of my time lifting weights and getting in shape for our swim race when I get out of here. I hope you're hitting the pool, because I want you in top form when we dive in that water together.

Your visitation form is good here too. Let's talk about that for a moment. In my mind and heart, you've already done more for me than I could have asked of you. You've given me back your friendship which to me is more valuable than you could know. Coming to see me in this cage isn't what matters, it's that you "would" that makes all the difference. Whether you see me wearing my own clothes or the state's—it doesn't matter. So don't worry about it, I'll see ya when I see ya! But I WILL see you. I'm not losing you again. We are going to be great friends again! What does your husband think about this? What does he like to do? Tell me more about him and your boys. And your sister—I remember meeting her at the swim meets in high school. If I recall correctly, she's a few years older than you and was out on her own by then.

Yes, both of my parents have passed away. I lost my mom shortly after I married Denise. She was at the grocery store one day and keeled over from a massive heart attack. It's really nice that you can remember my mom. She remembered you well. I guess it's hard to miss a redhead in the pool! I really miss her. In the darkness of the night, I talk to her and I can imagine her sitting next to me.

My mom knew me inside and out. She did not want me to marry Denise and she tried to discourage me from that decision. She knew I wasn't in love and that I was marrying Denise out of a sense of duty. She took a part of me with her when she died. On three different occasions, I've heard her voice out of the blue, always warning me of danger ahead. One time her voice came to me in the cockpit and alerted me to a small plane that had drifted into the military air space. Had she not alerted me, I would have hit that plane and who knows what would have happened. The second time I heard her voice she simply said, "Tony, look up." I was rappelling down a small cliff in Boulder when a rock broke loose and came barreling down. I was able to jump away just before the rock grazed my helmet. The third time was when I had the whole family in the car—Denise and I were fighting and my mom's voice said, "Stop!" At first, I thought she wanted me to stop fighting with Denise, but just then, a truck went through a red light. I slammed on the brakes and skidded to a stop–just inches from the truck as it drove by. Each and every time, her voice has saved me.

My dad passed away during my third year in prison after a long battle with Lou Gehrig's disease. He lost his ability to speak or write to me, so in some ways, he died long before his final breath. It took a lot of prayer to get me through. During that time, I had lost Mike as well because he wasn't speaking to me. He did not believe my innocence at first. Every now and then, we would connect on a phone call, but our conversations were stilted. Mike finally started coming around after I gave myself to God. I reached out to him in a long letter after my dad died and opened up my heart. I asked him to open his heart as well. After all, we had no family left but each other. In the last three years, he has been coming out to visit me once or twice a year. I always look forward to his visits, but at the same time, it tears me up. It reminds me so much of the past and all I have lost.

What about your parents–are they still around?

Well, I've only got two more courses to do to finish up my Bachelor's degree in Religious Studies/ Theology. I'm pretty excited about that. Then I'm planning to go for a Master's degree. There's a good chance I'll be able to complete the degree before I get out. I plan to go into some kind of ministry once I'm out. I want to return to prison and give hope to other inmates. After all, it is hope that keeps me going here along with God's help.

Thank you, Red, for the books you sent. I can't wait to read them. Say hi to your family for me. Take care now, more to follow.

Hugs, Tony

9.

Dear Tony,

I'm so sorry to learn that Steve passed away and that you've lost both parents. My heart goes out to you. Lou Gehrig's disease is a cruel one. My aunt battled that for seven years–longer than the average person lives–and she passed away two years ago. My parents are still around– they moved to Florida and we usually see them a couple of times throughout the year. They can't really travel anymore so they haven't been to our house in years. My dad has diabetes and it is starting to take a toll on him. My mom has a heart condition that limits her–she's often out of breath after a short walk. My sister lives a few hours away from me and we get together every other month. You remembered right; she's a lot older than me and had moved out of the house when I was in high school. I still haven't told her anything about you yet. I don't know why. I guess I'm just afraid that she might have the same reaction that Marie is having. I know I haven't shared this with you yet, but Marie has been a bit critical of me supporting you through this. She doesn't think it is healthy for us to connect again, especially with me being married and you in prison. So you can see why I haven't brought it up to my sister yet.

I know time must feel slow for you, but for me, it is spinning faster and faster with each day. I get sad when I think about the boys going off to college and me coming home to an empty house. Gary is so deep into his work lately that it's been me and the boys more often than not. The boys are starting to resent Gary for the amount of time he is spending at the office. He missed a major game recently and the boys aren't speaking to him right now. I honestly don't know what our marriage is going to be like once the boys are off to college. There's a part of my heart that feels empty because Gary and I are drifting apart.

Well, changing the subject, tell me about some of your travels? What was your favorite place that you've ever traveled to? For me, it was Belize. That island is so beautiful. Marie and I actually took a ladies only trip with two of our friends and stayed there for a week. This was actually before I met Gary, so I was young and single at that point. I danced with a local guy on the last night of the trip and fell in love. He had brown wavy hair down to his shoulders and dark piercing eyes. He was wearing a white, button down shirt and colorful board shorts. His name was Reef. He was a surfer by day and worked as a restaurant manager at night. We walked out to the beach and laid in the sand talking under the moonlight. I had one too many drinks and I was convinced that I was going to marry this guy. He was really sweet and we were kissing like mad. Marie and the other gals found us at that point and he took off—never to be seen again. So, who knows, I might have ended up married to a guy named Reef and living in Belize if it wasn't for the gals interrupting my exotic experience.

One country that surprised me was Germany. I never had any interest or desire to visit Germany. It wasn't a country on my Life List. Marie's assistant quit right before the trip and she convinced me to be her temporary assistant. We flew first class in one of those sleeper units and I fell asleep shortly after the plane took off. I woke up just as we landed.

In between different shoots, we had one day off. We rented a car and drove to Bonn and had lunch on the same street where Beethoven was born. It was a quaint little place and I felt like we were transported back in time. I still have the coffee mug that I purchased from a shop on that street and every time I take a sip, I'm transported back to that trip.

Gary and I took a trip to South Africa a year before the boys were born. He had always wanted to go on a safari. It was wonderful to see all the different animals in the wild–unlike when you see them in the zoos in America. We also visited an elephant sanctuary and saw three majestic elephants up close.

Tossing this letter in the mail before heading off to another busy three days at the hospital. Keep your head down and hang in there!

Hugs,

Shannon

Thanks, Red, for your letter. It came at a challenging time. I've been feeling very low lately. Dejected and discouraged–those are the words which come to mind. There's so much darkness in this place and the constant noise and chatter is getting to me. Some nights I cannot sleep because some of the guys stay up late and annoy the rest of us with their restlessness. Your letters are always the bright spot in this hellhole. I read them over and over every day.

It saddens me to learn that Marie hasn't been supportive of our connection. But...try not to be too hard on her. I understand her skepticism, after all, I've dealt with it on many occasions. I've lost so many friends over this situation.

I've been praying for what I need to make it through the last remaining months on this journey. I'm praying that the light at the end of this tunnel isn't another oncoming train. It has not been easy. Mike and his wife came to see me and we had "the talk" about what happens after I get out. Probation is going to be one long, drawn out affair.

Mike told me about Steve's funeral and the swim team guys who were there. Everyone asked where

I was and Mike beat around the bush on that one. He didn't want to have to explain why I was in prison, so he made up a story about me being out of the country. In my heart, I was there for my friend. His death still makes me cry and I'm ashamed of my situation keeping me from his side in his last hours.

Joshua got into a terrible fight here and ended up with a broken nose and several stitches. He's in the isolation unit right now and I'm not sure when he'll be able to get out. It's been a rough patch lately. Sometimes I just stay on my bunk bed and read your letters over and over. Your letters keep my sanity intact. It's so easy to get caught up in the misery of this place. I find myself longing to go "home," but I don't know where home is anymore. Sometimes I just lose my focus–one day blends into another and I lose all sense of time. Yes, I'm keeping my head down, though it isn't easy. There are times I want to lash out and give these inmates a good beating and put them in their place.

I really enjoyed hearing about your exotic experience with that guy in Beliza. It's good to know that you aren't opposed to kissing after all! (Ha!) So to answer your question, one of my favorite places to travel to was Saipan. I love that island. I don't like the touristy areas, instead, I like the local hiking trails that you won't find in the travel guides. Ok, I take it back, I do like the Grotto, many tourists go there. The Grotto is a hidden snorkeling and diving spot with turquoise blue water. It's not an easy place to get to–you have to navigate a rough staircase with over 100 steps. Quite a hike when you're hauling scuba gear!

There's a tiny little cafe that I went to every morning. The guy who owns it grew up on the island and he serves amazing food. When I close my eyes I can remember every delicious bite.

Another favorite place of mine is Kauai. That's the one place I'd love to go back to. There's a sense of peace on that island, especially when hiking up the many hills. If you've never been to Kauai, check out the Waimea Canyon. It is just as stunning (if not more) as the Grand Canyon but few people know about it.

So now I have a question for you: What are your favorite movies? What about your favorite authors? Obviously Kevin Hall, the author of that book you sent me, is one of your favorite authors. By the way, I'm loving that book, Aspire. The eleven words which Kevin outlines in the book are all great words. I think of all the words, "Passion" leaps out at me the most because it reminds me of you. Remember how we used to ride together on the trails? That was passion in action, and I don't mean the romantic kind. As corny as it is, I'll never forget the day we kissed on the cliff. Sorry to bring it up again. I know I confused the heck out of you because we were just friends. To be honest, I wanted something more but I didn't trust myself not to hurt your heart. Even though I was quite attracted to you, I valued our friendship beyond anything else and I didn't want to go down the romance road for fear of losing you. You and I could talk about anything for hours and I don't really have that kind of relationship with many other people.

So you're feeling sad about the boys growing up so fast? Seems like you blink and your babies aren't babies anymore. I miss my kids so much. Have you heard the Trace Atkins song, "You're Gonna Miss This?" A very profound song. I play it in my head all the time. Never fear though, the cycle will repeat itself with Grandma Shannon someday, so you've got that to look forward to. I hope I get the opportunity to be a Grandpa someday. Well, I want to get this in the mail. Looking forward to your next letter, Red. Say hello to the family for me.

Hugs, Tony

There it was again. The kiss. What would have happened if she had kissed him back that night? Would their friendship ever have blossomed into something more?

Ah, high school. A confusing time of personal

growth. Shannon thought back to that night at the top of the hill. Days after the kiss, Shannon felt a stirring inside of her and she imagined briefly what it would be like to make love to Tony. She knew his reputation of sleeping around and she didn't want to end up being "one of those girls" of his. Besides, their friendship had an intimacy of its own.

Taking a deep breath, Shannon wrote back–and asked Tony what would have happened if they had taken the leap beyond friendship.

10.

Dear Shannon,

Let's clear something up right away. Never think for one instant that I didn't want you. I most certainly did. You are not, nor have you ever been, "less" than the other girls I dated. In fact. you were so much more that I could not do to you what I did with the others, which was basically sleeping with them, breaking their hearts, and casting them aside. You were too special to me to allow that to happen. Even though we were close, I wanted to hold your heart intact. It meant that much to me. You are a keeper, Red, and I was foolish enough to pass on you.

Now about "liking you," did I ever give you the idea that I didn't? Or did you think that I was just after your body? If I wasn't in and out of a relationship with Lisa and a few others, I would not have hesitated in asking you out. Remember that kiss and how mad you were afterwards? I always felt like you were off limits after that. And remember all the times you came to my house for a swim? Do you know how hard it was for me to hold back? But I was not faithful to anyone back then. I was a breaker of beautiful things and I thank God that you were not one of them.

I do wish now that I would have made it clear to you then that you could've held your own against the other girls I was dating. High school can be a really cruel experience, ya know? Most girls didn't date me because they got to know me or because they thought I was sweet and kind, etc. No...most of them just wanted to "do Tony," like I was a stepping-stone to high school popularity or something. But I think you would have dated me because you saw something more substantial than a scrawny guy in a Speedo. You got to know me through all of our notes to each other. I regret overlooking you back then. I'm glad you're back in my life now. I missed ya!

One thing I also miss is flying. I know my career days are over—no one would ever let me fly commercially again. But I'll need to become friends with someone who has a small plane and will let me fly it. It's either that or become rich enough to buy my own plane! I always feel free in the air and I look forward to experiencing that feeling once again. I really think you should jump in a plane with me and let me show you the earth from up above. Heck, we could do some skydiving together! A little adrenaline rush to break up the monotony of life. What do you say, Red?

One idea that I'm toying with is opening my own business when I get out of here. Running my own business would be easier than trying to find a job as an ex-felon. I'm actually thinking about providing consulting services to churches so that they can open their doors to people like me–those who've had challenging paths to God. What do you think?

It has been so hot here lately and the stench is unbearable. One thing I cannot wait for is to sit in a place where the air conditioning is actually too cold!

Sending lots of loving hugs with this letter, Red!

Shannon grabbed her phone to call Marie. "You're not going to believe this!" she said. "Listen to what Tony wrote!" She read parts of the letter to Marie. "He liked me back then, he really did like me!"

"Girl, you sound like Sally Field when she won that Academy Award!" said Marie. "I always knew he liked you–I mean, come on, how many guys would pass notes in the hallway for a year and write letters while in the service? You were just too blind to see it."

"We were always friends, plus, I didn't have any confidence in high school. Tony was the popular one.

I couldn't see why he would even give me the time of day back then." Shannon could hear talking in the background. "Where are you now?"

"I'm in Key West. We just wrapped up another magazine shoot. Ben and I are grabbing a late dinner and then heading back to the hotel. He just proposed to his boyfriend–I tried to convince him to wait a year or two, but he didn't listen. He's still pretty much a kid! Tomorrow, we fly to California and then I'll be home for two weeks. I really can't wait for the break. I'm so sick of all this traveling." Ben was her current intern, a fresh-faced kid who graduated from Brooks Institute in California. Marie was in the middle of divorcing her second husband, a model she had met on one of her shoots. The marriage had lasted all of 18 months, and their relationship was a mistake from the start. Fortunately, she had made him sign a prenuptial agreement so the split was an easy one.

Shannon tried to brainstorm ways to help Tony fight his case and prove his innocence. A Google search turned up The Innocence Project–a non-profit organization which focused on providing help for inmates who were falsely incarcerated. Shannon gave them a call and explained Tony's case. After a lengthy conversation, a caseworker turned it down. Without DNA evidence, she said, there was no way they could get involved. Shannon called a couple of lawyers and the result was the same: it was not a case they were willing to take on.

Shannon fired off another letter, telling Tony about the Innocence Project and her efforts to help free him. She looked at the calendar–Tony's birthday was coming up. She went to the hall closet and grabbed a box filled with empty cards and found a blank birthday card. She thought back to her 16th birthday. Tony had sent her a small box in the mail. Inside was a beautiful sun and moon necklace. "No matter where we are, we share the same sun, and the same moon," Tony wrote. "Anytime you see the sun set and the moon rise, know that I'm thinking of you, too."

Shannon lost the necklace just a few months later while barrel racing at a rodeo. She spent hours looking over the dusty arena trying to find it, but to no avail. Shannon sealed the envelope and dropped it in the mailbox at the end of the driveway.

Red, thank you so much for the birthday card and the hug you sent with it. I can't believe that after all of these years–you remembered my birthday! This always makes me ask, "Who am I that you are mindful of me?"

It's a bummer you lost the necklace I gave you–but at least you were wearing it while doing something you loved!

I really enjoyed your letter reminiscing of your childhood. We had a lot more in common than

I realized. Mini-bikes and dirt bikes? We would have been great friends as kids. Since we weren't, I pledge to be a great friend to you now. I can just picture you hopping on your friend's dirt bike and riding back to your summer home–the look on your mom's face must have been priceless. I think your mom worried about you simply because you were a girl. There's not many girls who have the guts to ride dirt bikes or jump over a ramp on one! It's too bad your parents sold it right before you started high school. I would have loved to experience that lake with you.

There's still plenty of time to do exciting things as adults. I love rollercoasters too! My favorite is actually the old wooden ones. There's something nostalgic about riding on wood.

Did I ever tell you about the time I had my ear pierced? My Marine buddy, Larry, bought some silver hoop earrings for his wife. The day before he was set to fly home, he learned his wife was sleeping with one of their neighbors. We all went out drinking that night, to support Larry. The bar bill was high, but Larry didn't care, he kept buying everyone rounds. We had to take a cab back. The next morning, I woke up with one heck of a headache. My ear was on fire, there was blood on my neck. I looked in the mirror and saw a silver hoop dangling from my ear. I looked over at Larry's bunk–he had the other earring hanging out of his ear. He woke up, took one look at me and started laughing. "We look like pirates!" he said. Neither of us remembered who pierced our ears or where we were when it happened. We tossed those earrings in the garbage and cleaned up our ears. That was the one and only time I ever experienced women's jewelry on my body. Never again!

I want to thank you for your concern about my being here in prison. Thank you for contacting the Innocence Project and talking to lawyers. It warms my heart and I thank you for it, but there really is nothing you can do for me. I took a plea agreement foolishly when I thought I was protecting my daughters from the foster care system. For the first time in my life, I was afraid not for myself, but for them. I couldn't stand the thought of my two girls being separated and raised by strangers. My wife was a psychotic pill-eating drunk who couldn't keep a job and they had me believing they would take my kids and put them in the system. Even though now I know it was just a scare tactic— it cost me everything. I couldn't see straight back then. I was being beaten by the cops and they treated me like an animal. I would make the same decision every time, and they knew that. There was a time when I was in the county jail fighting my case and I got word that my step-daughter wanted to drop the charges. I thought everything was going to be ok. Had she dropped the charges and recanted her story, I could have sued the county for false imprisonment. The next time I *spoke with my lawyer, he said she changed her mind about it all. I thought we could use the fact that she at least wanted to drop the charges, but the State's Attorney denied that it was ever even talked about. There's so much more that happened throughout all of this, you wouldn't believe it. I don't believe it, and I'm writing to you from the recreation yard of a federal prison. Believe me, I've already explored all the options with my brother and his wife.*

The best thing is to just leave it alone and I'll leave here and start my life over. You want to help me out, Shannon? Then you just be one of the few people in the world who do believe that I could not possibly have done the things I was accused of. I know when we knew each other we were just kids in high school, but you've always held a part of my heart and I would never believe you were some kind of monster unless I took the time to find out for myself all of the facts.

The funny thing about all of this is the people who've professed to love me–they were the ones who were quick to believe the worst about me when this happened. Childhood friends, my brother, my ex-wife, my kids, military buddies... So, if you want to help me, then you continue to be one of those friends. I promise you won't be disappointed in doing so. I can be a pretty great guy! I still have a lot of love to give and friendship to extend. I just need some people to share it with. When I get out, I imagine it will be hard for me to find friends with this whole thing hanging over me. And meeting women—well, I can't even imagine that yet. I'm still hoping for love again. So I'm going to be needing you to help.

I'm going to wrap this up with a song I used to sing in choir; maybe I'll get to sing it for you one day:

"I've had some good days and I've had some hills to climb.

I've had some weary days and some sleepless nights

But when I look around and I think things over

All of my good days outweigh my bad days

And I, I won't complain

Sometimes the clouds hang low and I can barely see the road

And I ask a question, Lord, why so much pain?

But God's been good to me

When those weary eyes can't see,

That all of my good days outweigh my bad days

And I, I won't complain."

Love ya, Red!

Hugs, Tony

Shannon smiled. She heard the "I Won't Complain" song just the other day when one of her co-workers sang it after a long night shift where the paperwork piled up and the patient load was high. Now she could not get the song out of her head.

Shannon wrote the next letter in bits and pieces between breaks at work and while waiting in the dentist office. She told Tony about their upcoming Thanksgiving plans to take the boys to a local food kitchen and prepare food before coming home to a dinner of their own. She had picked up her old Bible again and started reading through the Proverbs. She asked him to share more about his military days and asked him if there was anything she could send him or if she could deposit money into a prison account to purchase extra items. Shannon figured if she could send him some small comforts, it would make the prison time go by faster.

11.

Hi Red,

My heart is hurting today. Joshua's daughter is getting married in a couple of hours and I can see how much it is paining him not to be there. He should be able to walk his little girl down the aisle. I know a small piece of him is dying inside. I can feel for him because I don't think I'll get to walk my girls down the aisle either. That's a scary feeling. If Joshua and I were keeping score, that would just be one more thing to add to the list of things taken from us because of lies. We could let that make us bitter men.

I chose not to let it make me bitter. I've got so little choice left to me, so I can't let it poison my heart— but it still hurts like hell. I'll be giving Joshua some space to deal with it all today. I'll just be there to listen if he wants to talk. Sometimes there are just no words and the two of us are comfortable in the silence between us. We are quite the tough guys, aren't we? This really sucks, Shannon. It seems like just when there's nothing left to lose, there's so much more to be lost. But "all of my good days outweigh my bad days" so I'll quit complaining now. The pity party has never been my style.

You asked me to share more about my military days, so here goes. After I completed basic training and spent two years on the ground, I went to flight school for six weeks for basic flight training. I transferred to Florida and did 22 weeks of primary flight training there. I trained on a variety of jets and helicopters. My only encounter with actual combat came from Desert Storm. My job was to run shipments of supplies and transport Marines. My military career has taken me to some wonderful places around the world. Before I got trapped with Denise, I was really enjoying the freedom of being single and having fun. Of course, some of that meant a girl in every port. (I'm kidding! Oh wait...there's SOME truth to that!)

Once my kid was born, all that changed. Suddenly I had a family and a new set of rules to play by. I was tied down, but I didn't mind it at all. I was ready. I advanced in my career and began training new pilots until I retired from the military. I look back at my military days with great appreciation. That choice took me to many fascinating places with great people.

Well, incarcerated life continues to get more and

more interesting here. I have to watch all of my stuff like a hawk. There's a lot of stealing going on and the fighting is escalating daily. It's getting harder and harder for me to keep my head down and stay out of the mess that's going on around me. Some days I have a strong urge to fight and to beat these punks to a pulp. Yesterday, one of the guys was beaten up–his eyes were swollen shut by the time the guards got to him. I'm pretty sure he's missing a couple of teeth as well and it looks like they broke his ribs.

The guards were really slow to show up. They don't really care. We are just bad people to them. The noise level alone is off the charts here even at night. The new kids coming in are younger and younger and they have some long rap sheets. We've got a lot of drug boys and gangbangers in here. They run in packs and they prey on anyone who shows a sign of weakness. I try to stay tough, but some days it just wears me down. It's going to be one hell of a long time before I get out of here. Yes, you can deposit money in a prison fund– this would allow me to purchase some extras–like candy. I still have a serious sweet tooth!

This year, I am so excited for Christmas for the first time in many years–because you've given me so much to look forward to. Christmas has always been my favorite time of the year. Now that I have God in my life and the Bible to live by, the significance of that special holiday is something

I keep deep in my heart. I'm thrilled that you've started to read your Bible again. I am honored to have inspired you to pick up the book. That makes me feel really good. Ya know, the wisest man in the Bible, besides Jesus, of course, once said in Ecclesiastes that "Better is the end of a thing than the beginning thereof and the patient in spirit is better than the proud in spirit."

So, tell me, what was Christmas like for you when you were growing up? I don't think we ever talked about the early years when we were together in high school. I have mixed memories of my holidays. On one hand, I love Christmas movies. My family always sat down every Christmas Eve and watched movies after dinner. My father however, created some Christmas memories that were less than stellar. On some of the holidays he would become very drunk and belligerent with my mom. They fought loud and hard. My dad was not always nice to my mom. He didn't hurt her physically, but he sure cut her down with his words. I can remember one Christmas where he passed out in the middle of a movie. We were all sitting around the couch and my dad was out like a light. My mom put a blanket over him and we all went to bed. But for me, movies were always my escape. I especially love Holiday Inn, It's a Wonderful Life and believe it or not, that cheesy movie-- Christmas with the Kranks. A little humor always goes a long way.

What about you? What are your favorite Christmas movies?What are some of the traditions you've created with your kids?

I have included two pictures of my kids with this letter. The first one is a picture of Julie and Amanda in elementary school. The second picture is the last picture I took with the three girls before all this mess happened. As you can see, Taylor looks as happy as can be. She certainly doesn't look like a teen who is being hurt by a stepfather. Of course, I no longer have any pictures of Denise. I consider it a good riddance that she is not in my life. I do regret that first night meeting her in the bar, but I don't regret my children being born. Life is definitely richer for having my children in it.

Well, it's time for me to get to bed and get this in the mail. Can you send the pictures back as they're all that I have of my kids. I have nothing else-- just those two pictures. I always look forward to your letters, Red. I wish you could feel how deeply I appreciate you.

Love, Tony

Shannon's memories of Christmas with her family were very good ones. Her parents loved celebrating the holidays and they always did it in style. Shannon and Cathy grew up in a sprawling ranch with a full basement. Every year, the basement was filled with family and friends. Her mom was an interior decorator, so the dining room table was a beautiful work of art. The Christmas tree towered almost two stories high in the cavernous, A-frame living room. Shannon's father often grumbled about the money she spent every year but her mom was frugal enough to score her decorations from second-hand shops and garage sales. She was an excellent cook as well and the plates were graced with concoctions out of French cookbooks with names she couldn't pronounce.

Gary's family was scattered in different states, so every other year, they alternated between families. This year, they were spending Christmas in Oceanside, California, where Gary's older brother, Alan, owned a home right on the beach. Alan and his wife, Jenni, owned an insurance company. Jenni was Alan's second wife and they had one child together. Johnny was the same age as the twins and the three of them were close.

The twins always looked forward to Christmas on the west coast. When the conditions were right, the three boys often went out surfing on Christmas morning, braving the cold waters with full wetsuits. On Christmas Eve, they gathered around the fire on the beach and watched the sun go down. It was a stark contrast to the holidays back home.

Gary's younger brother Ralph often hit the bourbon so early that by the time they lit the first log, he was sound asleep in a lawn chair. The boys loved him–

he was the fun uncle who could wrestle them in the sand and tickle them until they asked for mercy. He had never married and as far as they knew, he wasn't dating anyone. He worked for an advertising agency as a copywriter and his generous salary and bonuses provided him with a comfortable income. He lived frugally, preferring to spend his money on his ever-growing collection of expensive art.

Shannon went down to the beach the day after Christmas to write Tony a letter. The sun was just beginning to rise and there was a chill in the damp air. She sat on a large boulder and listened to the gentle roll of the waves. The ocean was mostly calm and no one else was on the beach.

Shannon wrote and wrote. The words seemed to flow as she filled up page after page. She told Tony about the single article she found on the internet and how he saved a civilian from a house fire. *Tell me more about that*, she wrote. *Tell me the stuff that's not in the article. And what about Mike–how did he finally come around? What was Christmas like with your kids?* Shannon wrote several pages telling Tony about the many Christmas memories she had as a child. She described their Christmas in California–telling him about Ralph, Alan, Jenni, and Johnny. This year, Ralph gave the boys brand-new Macbooks. The boys were sitting on the couch, deep into exploring the features and downloading apps.

On Christmas morning, Shannon called her sister

Cindy and casually mentioned that she had heard from Tony. She wasn't ready to share the details about his prison sentence. Cindy didn't ask many questions, to Shannon's relief.

"What's this I hear about you having an ex-boyfriend in prison?" Ralph plopped down on the couch next to her.

"Have you been talking to Gary?'

"Yeah. He says you've been writing to this guy. What's the deal here?"

"First of all, he's not an 'ex-boyfriend.' He's a friend I knew well in high school. Second, he was falsely implicated and beaten to the point he just gave in and took a plea bargain. I'm just writing to him as a friend, nothing more."

"I sure hope it's nothing more. You hear stories about women writing to men in prison and they end up leaving their families–then the guy turns out to be a con artist. I would hate it if that happened to you."

"Ralph, thanks for your concern, but this is not that kind of situation."

"Just sayin, ya know?"

On the way to the airport, Shannon dropped off another letter to Tony.

Red,

Thank you for the Christmas card and the books you sent. Every book is a lifesaver for me–they help me pass the time here. So sorry that you had a family member question writing to me–you're going to just have to develop a thick skin when it comes to our connection. Other people simply won't understand what we have between us.

Now about that fire...I was on my way home when I noticed the whiffs of smoke coming out down the road. When I rounded the bend, I realized it was coming out of a side window of a sprawling ranch home. I got out of the car and knocked at the front door–no answer. When I walked around the side, the flames were flickering in the window. I called 911 and ran around to the back. I decided to break in just in case someone was trapped inside. The smoke was getting thick at this point. I yelled and yelled and suddenly I heard a voice, "I'm in the back bedroom!"

Of course, I had no idea where to go, so I kept yelling and asking him to guide me. At this point, I was crawling on the floor. I got into the kitchen and grabbed a dishtowel, wetted it, and used it as a mask. A few more feet of crawling and I found the back bedroom. Turns out, the guy was elderly and needed a cane to walk. He had laid down for a nap when the fire started. An electrical outlet had overloaded–he was running a very old air conditioner and the cord was frayed and bent.

By this point, there was no way to get back out through the back door so we had to escape through the window. The fire truck arrived just as I carried him across the yard. Unfortunately, his two cats perished in the fire. I debated whether or not to go back in and try and find his pets, but the fire was roaring at that point. The old house went up quickly in flames.

Thanks for sending back the pictures of my kids. I'm glad you got to see what they look like. I wish I had more pictures with me, especially of when they were little. I miss them dearly–it's almost as if they died. I've often wondered if they would write to me if they weren't so much under their mom's influence. She has truly turned them against me. I'm not sure what stories she told them, but it must have really impacted them.

Christmas with my kids was a magical time. I think it was the only time of year when things were good. Every year, we participated in Operation Christmas, a local effort to collect toys for those in need. A local farm donated hams so we drove around in the days before Christmas and dropped off packages to families. Just watching the smiles on their faces was a gift.

As for Denise, I don't remember if I told you everything about my criminal situation yet, but during the bombardment of accusations flung against me, she accused me of forcing myself on her and physically abusing her. I also had the charges of abusing my kids thrown in.

Red, those accusations just about killed me. I had never laid a hand on my wife nor my children. I used to spank Julie when she was a toddler--until one day I realized I was raising her to behave with violence. I stopped right then. Julie was so young she wouldn't even remember this.

As for Mike, in the beginning, we had a rift between us. With this whole mess, I know he was embarrassed and I felt like I let him down or shamed him. When it first happened, he stopped contacting me. I think he figured I was guilty, so he stayed away. My letters were returned unopened. So I stopped writing to him and for a long time, I figured I pretty much was dead to everyone I loved. Mike sent me a short letter when our dad died and I wrote him back. I didn't hear back from him. Then the following Christmas, he sent me a card. Finally, he began to call me once a month and most of our conversations were pretty cordial. The first time he visited me in prison, I hugged him so long and hard. I was so starved for my family and human touch.

I started sharing my journey of faith with him and I think he finally believed me that I did not do the things I was accused of. We slowly began repairing our relationship and became brothers again. We try not to talk about the past because it's too painful. We keep our conversations light and we don't talk about anything deep. In some ways, I lost my brother because I used to be able to talk to him about anything. Sometimes I feel like I'm walking on eggshells with him. I am not crazy about his wife and she definitely doesn't like me. They tried for years to have kids but that never happened. I had hoped they would adopt at one point so that my kids would have cousins, but that wasn't something they wanted to pursue. I try hard to hang on to what we have now, because he's my brother and he's the only blood I have left. If I don't have him in my corner, I have nothing. Well, not so true–because I have you back in my life too!

Big hugs, Tony

12.

"How do you feel about me visiting Tony in prison?" Shannon asked Gary one night.

Gary looked up in surprise. "Well, I'm not too sure about that," he said. "You'll be going into a dangerous place with other felons. I don't think I want you doing that."

"Gary, the poor guy hasn't had any visitors in a long time," she said. "All of his friends think he's guilty. For several years, his own brother shunned him. I mean, put yourself in his place, wouldn't you be grateful if someone, anyone, came to visit you in prison?"

Gary shrugged. "If you are comfortable doing this, I suppose it would be okay. I just don't like the idea of you going into a place like that," he said.

"It's only four hours from here and just 45-minutes from my sister's house. I can leave on a Friday and stay with Cathy. Visiting days are only on the weekends so I would go in on Friday, hang with Cathy, and then come right back."

"Well, I'm not going to stop you, but I don't think you should make a habit of this. The boys need you."

"I know. I just want to give him some support with a visit. I won't go overboard with it."

"That's fine. I've got a couple of golf outings coming up so can you work around those? I don't want to leave the boys home alone on a weekend."

"Yeah. Email me your calendar for next month and I'll see if Cathy will be home as well. And don't forget, I have the Girl's Night Out tomorrow. You'll need to go to the boys' games without me."

"Why are you scheduling a girl's night out when the boys have a game?"

"It was the only night this month that Marie was in town. Besides, you didn't have anything planned tomorrow so the timing worked out so that you could go to the games. You've been golfing and working so much that you've missed a couple of games. For once, it's my turn to have some fun."

"I'm not complaining, I was just surprised you planned a night out when the boys have games."

"Now you know how I feel. I've been doing the boy's games myself the last couple of times. Just deal with it, Gary. I'm going to go sit out back. It's just too cold in here with the air conditioner blasting."

"Well, you're wearing a sleeveless t-shirt. Go put on

something warmer."

Shannon grabbed a notebook and her sunglasses from the desk and stepped out the sliding door into the backyard. She immediately realized she was thirsty. She went back inside to pour a glass of green tea and squeezed half of a lemon into it. A lone seed fell into the tea. Shannon fished it out with a fork and tossed it into the trash can.

The Texas heat hit her when she stepped out again. The warmth felt good on her cold skin. She took a sip of tea and sat down to write.

Dear Tony,

Sorry that it's been a while since I wrote. I've been taking some extra shifts at work because two of the nurses are out on maternity leave. One of the nurses also lost a sister to cancer, so it's been rough at work. There's really not too much new around here. I talked to Gary about the idea of visiting you and he's fine with it. He's not too happy about me going into a prison, but I'm sure it's not much of a big deal. My sister Cindy now knows and she hasn't expressed much of her opinion. She's always been supportive of me, though. She lives near the prison so I plan to stay at her house. Once I figure out which weekend, I'll let you know.

I'm going out with the girls this weekend and I'm really looking forward to it. I haven't spent much time with Marie lately because she's been doing one photo shoot after another. It's a miracle we were all able to schedule the same day together. There are four other girls going with us. We've been friends for about fifteen years with three of them, Penny, Jasper, and Courtney. Leanna joined us about five years ago. Leanna and Marie are the single ones and they don't have any kids. Penny has four kids, Jasper has two step-children, and Courtney adopted twins from Russia. Courtney's kids are deaf, so we've all learned a little sign language. We are quite the eclectic bunch, but it works. Penny and Leanna are often on each other's nerves, but most of the time they get along–if we keep them sort of apart. We are going out for sushi and I'm sure there will be a few saki bombs in there too. None of us drive on our nights out–either the hubbies drop us off or we take Uber. It's always a fun night out. I am looking forward to my girl time.

Well, gotta finish up here and go food shopping. I'm sure Gary and the boys would basically starve if I didn't plan everything out. They're so used to me doing things for so long. It will be interesting when the boys leave home–I probably won't know what to do with myself by then–all that time to myself!

'Til next time.

Love, Shannon

Shannon was looking forward to the night out with the girls. It was a wonderful way to kick back and escape from the everyday stuff. The six of them were pretty close. Whenever she talked about Tony, the group listened quietly for the most part.

With the exception of Penny. Penny didn't approve at all.

"You're married–you have no business writing to a man in prison. Trust me, no good will come of this. If I were you, I would stop writing to him."

"Gary knows about this. I have nothing to hide. Tony and I were good friends in high school and that's all this is, a friendship."

"It doesn't matter. How do you even know if he's innocent like he claims?"

"I'm just going by my instincts and the stuff that Mike has told me about Tony's situation. Surely if his brother backs him up, then that says a lot, doesn't it?"

Penny shrugged. "I just don't want to see you get hurt or waste your time on someone who has no future ahead of him. Even when he gets out, it will be a rough life. No one hires felons who serve time. You're just wasting your time with him."

"Maybe it's not a waste of time–it's kinda like a safe fantasy," Jasper chimed in.

"What do you mean?" Marie asked.

"Well, think about it. A sexy guy locked away in prison. All sweaty with bulging muscles. Shannon can mentally screw him all she wants–Gary doesn't have to know."

"Oh geez, Jasper, do we really have to go there?" Marie threw a crouton at her.

"Come on, Shannon, you've been telling us how lonely you are in your marriage and now you've got this Tony guy in your life–you expect us to believe that you're not shagging him in your mind?"

Shannon threw her head back and laughed. "Shagging? I haven't heard that word in years!"

"I screw Brad Pitt in my mind every Saturday night, just saying." Jasper grinned.

Shannon,

So good to hear from you. Every day, I excitedly wait for a letter to arrive. It gives me something to look forward to. I've been busy writing some papers for the Theology degree I'm working on. It took all of my stamps to send it out. I sent a letter to Mike to ask for more money in my account but he was in the middle of a move to a new home so nearly a month passed before he finally deposited the funds.

Mike's wife, Sarah, isn't too crazy about me. She's been married to Mike for twelve years and they have no kids. She's an environmental engineer and she works on a solar farm. I think she's part of the reason why Mike turned against me from the beginning, but I can't be sure. In any case, we've made our peace and we have worked to keep the family bond intact.

How did your Girl's Night go? Did you have fun? I sure miss how you girls smell. Sometimes at night, I close my eyes and remember the familiar smells of perfume. I also miss the smell of home. It's been so long since I've been to my childhood home, but I can remember the distinct smell of "home." It's a mixture of sunshine, fabric softener, and home cooking. Yeah, if you can imagine how sunshine must smell! That familiar warmth of the sun coming through the windows at home. This place is so dark, drab and dreary. I have to escape in my mind, or I will literally go insane. There have been many days I imagine myself in a plane again, flying high over the mountains and seeing the rivers below. I've spent the last several years searching the Bible trying to make sense of all that's happened. I can tell you that I believe God is real and He has a plan for each of us–and his plan is perfect, even though it may not seem like it at the time. We may not understand His plan, but it all happens for a reason. One day I'll be out of here creating a new path and a new life–perhaps the 'reason' may show up then.

Sometimes in the night, when the tears come, I just can't stop them. I used to wonder how my heart could hurt so bad and continue to beat, yet still it does. I used to ask God, in my foolishness, to let it stop beating. I used to think no one would care. I know better now. I've got faith that I will see my parents and Steve again. Heaven is a real place.

So tell me, Shannon, what is faith like for you? Do you and your family go to church? What about the Bible? Is this something you read often? I hope you don't mind these questions. I'm just truly curious. My own journey of faith has been something which sustained me through this hell, so I can't imagine my life without God in it.

That is really wonderful news about the possibility of you coming to visit me here. I look forward to seeing you, yet, I don't dare get my hopes up until you know for sure. Is the hubby ok with it?

I love you, Red. I hope you don't mind me saying this. Since I've been in here, I realize time is so precious and you should always love others—and tell them this—for you never know when you might not see or hear from them again. Thank you for your friendship.

Hugs, Tony

Shannon was trembling when she put the letter down. *I love you.* She hadn't heard those words from Gary in a long time. The words from Tony leapt off the page. She knew it was just a gesture of love tied to friendship, but the words warmed her heart. Shannon stared at the words again. *I love you.* The words were so strange coming from Tony. Shannon didn't want to read too much into it, because after all, they were just friends. Back in high school, she would have given anything to hear those words from him, especially if he wasn't dating Lisa.

Faith was not an easy topic for Shannon to discuss. She had long ago abandoned the regular practice of going to church and it had been years since she opened her Bible. Even though they had stopped going to church as a family when the boys were young, Shannon continued to pray occasionally. She believed in God; after all, He was the voice within that guided her through the years.

Dear Tony,

I'm really glad that God didn't listen to you and take you home. You are definitely on this earth for a reason. The journey you're going through will someday reveal itself with the "why." For now, you must simply trust in the process. Trust in God is something I'm learning anew each day.

The Girl's Night Out was just what I needed. We went to our favorite sushi place and ordered just about everything possible. I imbibed far more than I wanted to, but it was nice to escape from the everyday routine and just unwind with the girls. Everyone asked about you, and I shared what I could without telling them all the details. Most of them are pretty supportive, but of course several of them are skeptical, like Penny, and especially Marie. She's been quite vocal about her disdain of my involvement with you, but most of the time she keeps her opinions tempered down. Fortunately, she kept quiet that night and we had a pleasant time. It was Penny who was the most vocal that night. She thinks I'm wasting my time.

I filled out all the paperwork for the prison visit and sent it back. I plan to stay at Cathy's house when I visit you. It will be kind of weird to see each other after so many years, but I have no doubt that we'll pick up our friendship easily again. Writing these letters feels like high school all over again.

I am curious, what happened with you and Lisa after high school? When did you break up?

Well, in other news, I received a nice, unexpected award this week. About a year ago, I started volunteering with an organization that trains service dogs for blind people. Whenever a new dog is matched with someone, we walk alongside to ensure that the dog and the blind person build a trusting, reliable relationship before they return home on their own. I enjoy the work and I have met some really cool people as a result. By the way, if you want a book recommendation, I have to give two paws up for Marley and Me. If you can't get it from your prison library, let me know. I'll send you a copy.

Now what about movies, what are some of your favorites?

Sorry this letter is a short one, I've got four 12-hour shifts coming up and have to grab some sleep.

Hugs,

Shannon

Shannon closed her eyes and tried to imagine what it would be like to be trapped in a cell year after year. She put down the pen and grabbed a bottle of Estee Lauder "Beautiful" and sprayed it on the letter. Instantly, she regretted it. What if he took it the wrong way? What if the perfume would make it harder for him to deal with his days in prison? She went back and forth and then shoved the letter in the envelope. The small things in life could make a difference. Perhaps this would bring him a little comfort.

Dear Red,

Wow girl, do you smell good! That perfume you sprayed on your letter is amazing! I read your letter shortly before lights out last night and put it under my pillow. This morning, I woke up and I could still smell your perfume. That's nice! What kind is it? Thank you for that. It's been so long since I've had a nice scent around here.

The first time Mike and his wife, Sarah, came to see me, I hadn't seen them in a few years. I hugged him for a good five minutes. When I went to hug Sarah, I had forgotten what a woman felt like. She smelled so good and was nice and soft in all the right places. That's when I realized how much I missed the opposite sex! I guess I've blocked it out. I haven't had sex of any kind since I was last with my ex-wife. It's been quite the long "dry spell" but I try not to think about it. This is my journey right now and I just have to deal with it.

Well, my dissertation turned out well considering it was hand-written. My topic was about applying scripture to my life in order to change it from a skeptical outlook to that of a believer. It took forever to write and I put a lot of effort into it. I'm really proud of what I wrote. Since I've come to prison, I've heard hundreds of preachers say this or that about the Bible or Jesus. I decided to find out what it says for myself. I'm not a religious person either. Jesus didn't teach religion. Fault can be found in every single denomination if you look for it. I believe in God because I know what he's done for me. I know the prayers that have been answered. YOU happen to be one of those prayers.

Anyway, for more good news—the University must have liked what I wrote because I received my B.A. degree! I'm going to dive right in and start working on my Master's next. School keeps my mind off of things around here and it gives me something to work for. After all, I've got nothing better to do with my time. It drives me crazy when I see the others just sitting around waiting to pick on the next victim. They could be using their time for something gainful, but instead, they choose to waste it.

Red, that is wonderful about your award with the service dog organization. That is so cool that you train dogs for the disabled. Where do you find the time to do all you do? Nursing, volunteering, and raising two boys? Plus you're taking the time to write to an old friend in prison. Have I told you that I'm proud of you? Even if I didn't love you, I'd be proud just to know you! I hope you feel appreciated in all that you do.

Thanks for your book recommendations. I have not read "Marley and Me" but I'll be sure to request that in the library here. Yes, growing up, we had several dogs. My first dog was an Old English Sheepdog named Shep. Hair everywhere! When I was five, I was teasing the poor thing and he decided to nip me in the ear. I ended up with seven stitches. Shep died two years later. My heart was so broken. I told my mom I could never love another dog again. Six months later, mom brought home a tiny toy poodle. I think they call them "teacup dogs" nowadays. We named her Goldie, because she had the most translucent coat which shimmered like gold when the sun hit her.

At first, I gave my mom a lot of grief about buying a poodle. I mean, come on, what young boy wants a tiny dog? No, we want the labs, the german sheperds and the pit bulls. But Goldie ended up sleeping with me every single night, much to my mom's disappointment. She thought Goldie was going to be "her" dog but she ended up being mine. She wanted nothing to do with Mike, and he felt the same way about her. A few years later, Mike came home with a stray-- a mutt we named Riley. Riley and Goldie never got along, so we kept Riley outside a lot.

Unfortunately, Riley got out of the backyard one day and was hit by a car. Goldie ended up with diabetes and died just before my freshman year of high school. That's why you never knew me with pets. My parents never had another dog after that. As soon as I get out of this place, I'm going to the pound and I'm gonna parole me an "inmate" just like me. I figure I'm going to be lonely when I get out, what better way to find companionship than a loyal pet? How about you–what pets did you have while growing up? I seem to remember a variety of creatures at your house during high school.

As for movies, my favorite movie is "Trading Places." It makes me laugh every single time. I've seen it dozens of times. I also like "Cast Away," that Tom Hanks movie where he ends up on an island talking to Wilson, the volleyball. In many ways, that's how I feel right now. Instead of talking to a volleyball, I talk to the Big Guy. He's my Wilson. I do have one beef with that movie though–what was in that last package that he delivered? I wish the gal would have opened it. Wouldn't it be funny if it was something he could have used–like a silverware set, some clothes, or a warm blanket? Oh, and I loved Forrest Gump, too! I think any movie with Tom Hanks in it is always good.

Thank God for you, Red. Your letters give me something to look forward to. You are such a wonderful blessing in my life and I love you for it. Thank you.

Hugs, Tony

Cast Away. Trading Places. Those were Shannon's favorite movies as well as Forrest Gump. What were the chances?

As for pets, Shannon grew up with a beagle named Bingo, four cats, two parakeets, four hamsters and lots of goldfish. At one point in her life, she briefly considered going to medical school to become a vet. Somewhere along the way, Marie convinced her nursing was a safer, more "sane" route in medicine. "Animals don't pay well," she said. Her sister, Cathy, became a Master Groomer and renovated an old van into a mobile grooming center.

13.

Shannon woke up early on Saturday to the rare sound of rain on the roof. The gray clouds matched the melancholy mood she was in. She slipped out of bed quietly and went into the den. She had been so busy lately that the house was in disarray. A bin of rags and dusting spray sat on her desk. She had planned to clean the room earlier in the week but the boys had basketball games for three nights in a row.

Two stacks of books sat on her desk because there was no room on the book shelves to add any more. Gary grumbled from time to time and begged her to stop buying books. "All the money you spend on books, we could be putting that in savings. Besides, that's what libraries are for," he said.

Shannon wished she could mail some of her books to Tony, but the prison had a strict policy of sending books from online stores only. She sat down at the desk and ordered two of her favorite books to be sent to the prison. She knew Tony would appreciate the books. He loved to read. Gary was the opposite--he liked his information fast, and on the web.

"Mom."

Shannon was surprised to see Zach at the door. He usually slept until noon on the weekends.

"What are you doing up so early?"

"Can I talk to you?"

"Sure, honey. Here, sit down."

"Mom, who are you getting letters from? I keep seeing you getting mail."

At first, Shannon didn't know what to say. How was she going to explain a complicated situation to her son?

"Zach, you know how you are best friends with Cassandra?"

"Yeah."

"Well, the guy who is writing to me is Tony. You may have heard me mention him here and there."

"The guy you used to ride horses with?"

"Yes, that's him. He's writing from a prison–he is doing time for a crime he did not commit. We got in touch recently and have been writing back and forth. As friends, of course. Your father knows–I am not hiding anything."

Zach let out a sigh of relief. "I was kinda worried you were having an affair with someone. You and dad have been fighting so much lately."

"Look son, you have nothing to be worried about. I most certainly am not having an affair–I am giving support to a friend. It's nothing more than that. Tony and I were good friends in high school and we've simply picked up the friendship again. Go hop back in bed, it is Saturday and there's nothing scheduled until the late afternoon."

"All right, thanks for listening, Mom."

"Come here, son." Shannon gave Zach a long hug. "I love you, kiddo."

Red,

What a wonderful surprise you sent! They called me up to the front desk and that usually means a specimen check so I show up and get handed a cup and provide the "evidence"-only to find out I was getting a delivery of books instead! Thank you, girl! I can't wait to dive into them. Books help me pass the time here in a positive way. I want you to know that the books will always be on the shelves no matter where I live. A reminder of something good coming from the worst time of my life: finding you again! You've reminded me of so much I've forgotten over the years in this dark place and you've given me hope.

I'm glad you feel comfortable talking about anything with me. Mike is probably the only person who knows me on the deepest level, although I shared a lot with you in that short time in high school. I always felt like I could trust you with my feelings and I felt safe opening up to you.

Now, about all those girls in high school, yeah, I slept around a bit, but not to the extent that everyone assumed. I loved to flirt, but it didn't end up the way the rumors came out. My heart was with Lisa, only I didn't really realize it at the time. We fooled around for the longest time and despite my reputation with the ladies, we didn't sleep together until the night of junior prom. My mom drove a wedge between us. She didn't like me spending time with Lisa and she was pretty vocal about it. Whenever I spent time with Lisa it was always at her house. The problem was, Lisa and I were as different as night and day. We didn't have a lot in common and she didn't share my love of horses like you did. But in many ways, I loved her. I just didn't know it at the time.

My mom definitely did not like Denise and tried hard to talk me out of marrying her. She felt strongly it was a mistake and in hindsight, she was right. Our wedding wasn't much of a wedding at all, we got married at the courthouse. Denise's parents were there, along with her sister and two cousins. I had my parents there and Mike–and of course, the kids. That was it. It was one of those "throw it together" weddings and we didn't put much thought into it. We just wanted to make it legal as a family. We left the kids with my parents and took off for Siesta Key for our honeymoon. We only stayed there three days and two nights but we never left the resort. That was actually probably the best time in our entire marriage. We were relaxed and stress-free for the first time. As soon as we got back home, life went into a routine.

Now back to Lisa. Just before I met Denise, I actually tried to get back together with Lisa. I finally woke up to what my heart was saying all along–that Lisa was the one I should have married. She came out to see me once. I was home on leave and we booked a hotel room in South Carolina for a week. I remember getting up one morning–the sun was just coming up through the blinds and shining softly into the room. I rolled over and just watched her sleeping. She looked so peaceful, almost angelic. That week was one of the best weeks of my life. There was a little voice inside of me saying, "If you let her go, you'll never be happy."

Well, that voice was right, but I chose to ignore it at the time. I wasn't ready to commit to her or anyone at the time. Had I listened to that little voice, perhaps I would be happily married to her today. I had my shot at her twice, and I blew it away. At that time, Lisa was living with a guy and she went back home to him. She was waiting for an answer from me, but it was an answer that I wasn't ready to give. Right after that, I got Denise pregnant and the noose was set. Lisa was so mad at me when I told her and she blew up at me. Rightfully so. I screwed up, big time. Lisa went on to get married to the guy she was living with and now she has three kids. I never talked to her again. I only heard bits and pieces through the grapevine over the years. I have no idea if she's happy, but I do include her in my daily prayers. I'm grateful for the little bit of happiness that we had together.

So, Red, that was a lesson for me–to learn to listen to that voice within. I now know that "voice" is God speaking to me and I have learned to listen to Him. Funny thing, well, I guess not so funny, but several years into my marriage with Denise, my mom ended up apologizing to me for driving that wedge between me and Lisa back then. It was far too late by then, but it was nice to have her blessing about it.

Now about me and you–we have something so incredibly special that it's beyond anything I could ever dream up. You've always been there for me and you're very precious to me. It goes beyond any relationship I've ever had in my life. I won't ever take our friendship for granted again. Every night, before I go to sleep, I keep you in my prayers and I give thanks for our connection and that you had the strength and willingness to reach out. I love you for that, Red. I pray that Gary understands and I thank him for his generosity in sharing you.

Love, Tony

Shannon put the letter down and closed her eyes.

Listen to the voice within? Right now, her own feelings, thoughts, and emotions were in a jumble. Was she intentionally drifting away from Gary? Should she be focusing on her own marriage instead of spending time writing to Tony?

And why did her heart skip a few beats every time she received a letter from him?

The night before, Marie called and their conversation was not a pleasant one. She lashed out at Shannon and told her she was foolish to continue her involvement with Tony.

"I don't trust him," Marie said. "The likelihood of him truly being innocent is really slim. I'm not sure I believe that bullshit about signing a plea agreement--it sounds a little too put together. I think you're getting in over your head on this, Shannon. I love you and I'm not afraid to tell you that you're going down a dangerous road. You've got a family. Stop wasting your time with him."

"Come on, Marie, you know I wouldn't have gotten this far into it if I didn't believe he was innocent. I know he was framed. He's a good guy. You're just going to have to trust me on this."

"This is one time where I think your trust system is screwed up, girl. You're not seeing this with objective eyes. You're just in too deep to see your way out of this."

"Look, I appreciate your concern but we've gone

over this enough times that it's become a wedge between us. Can't we just agree to leave it alone?"

"Fine. I've gotta run here and catch a flight to London. I'll see you when I get back."

From the tone of her voice, Shannon knew it was anything but fine.

14.

The sun was already beating down hard when Shannon left Cathy's house at 7:30 in the morning. Beads of sweat were forming as she waited for the air conditioning to kick in. The prison was just 45-minutes from her sister's house.

Shannon pulled into the parking lot and turned off the engine. The sharp, double rolls of barbed wire glistened in the morning sun. Patches of dull green grass snaked around barren spots in the prison yard. The bright orange of the prisoner uniforms stood out in stark contrast. She sat in the car and took it all in. In a few minutes, she was going to be on the other side of that barbed wire.

Shannon pulled down the mirror and brushed her bangs. She applied a pale pink lipstick and studied herself in the mirror. The tell tale signs of midlife were beginning to show on her face. The deep lines etched in her forehead were carved from years of both stress and laughter.

Shannon grabbed her license, some photos, and

twenty dollars. She stuffed them in her back pocket and got out of the car. She locked the door and headed toward the entrance.

At the front window, a guard slipped her a piece of metal with a number stamped on it. Shannon stood in the waiting area and listened to the banter around her. There were quite a few toddlers running around. She tried to imagine the fathers inside, waiting to spend time with their women and children. She watched as one mom balanced a baby on her hip with a wailing toddler clinging to her leg. With a sigh, she reached down and picked up the toddler. In an instant, both children were screaming. The toddler slid back down to the floor. The mom bribed the toddler with a Ziplock bag of Oreos but the child threw himself on the concrete floor and only screamed louder.

When her number was called, Shannon stepped into the building. It took a moment for her eyes to adjust. A guard motioned her to the desk. "Which inmate?" he asked.

"Tony Ambrose."

"Ok, since you're a first time visitor, we need to take your fingerprints. The next time you come in, you can swipe your fingers through. I need your driver's license."

Shannon waited as the guard processed all her information after meticulously inking every finger on each hand.

"Ok, you're cleared. Go ahead to the pat down room number two."

A plump, female guard met her at the door and they walked into a narrow room with a wooden bench bolted to the wall.

"I'm going to give you a quick pat-down. Hold your arms out to the side."

Shannon could hear the boredom in her voice. Probing through female bodies was just another typical routine task in her day.Shannon closed her eyes and tried not to feel the unfamiliar hands probing every inch of her body.

"All right. You can go."

Shannon walked through a double set of doors into a building reserved for visitors. She gave a stack of paperwork to the guard at the door.

"You're here for Tony Ambrose? Okay, have a seat." He motioned to a row of chairs along the wall. There was only one available seat, between a young adult with multiple piercings and a matronly grandmother who looked as uncomfortable as Shannon felt. She squeezed in between the two of them.

The noise from 30 prisoners and their families was deafening. Some of the men were fresh out of high school. In the corner, a gray-haired man sat stone-faced across from a woman who was trying to cajole a smile out of him.

A shriek pierced through the din and Shannon caught a glimpse of the same toddler throwing a fit on the floor. One of the prisoners tried to calm him down. Shannon assumed he was the father.

Out of the corner of her eye, Shannon saw Tony emerge from a doorway, A wave of shock hit her. Everything was different about him. The wavy locks were gone; replaced by a salt-and-pepper crew cut. In her mind, she saw the Tony she remembered in high school. Now a stranger was walking toward her, but as he came closer, she saw the familiar blue eyes looking right at her. Tony made his way through the tables with a big grin.

"Red!"

He wrapped her in a hug.

"I can't believe you're here!"

He stepped back and looked at her.

"I've spent a lot of time thinking back on our memories. You look just as I remember you."

Shannon blushed. Tony lead her to a table and they sat down.

"I can't believe the chain of events that lead us here," she said.

"Well, this is definitely not the circumstances that I would want a reunion, but we'll have to make the best of it. I'm just so happy to see you. This place is sometimes so dark and dreary. You're like a fresh breath of air. I'm telling you, when I get out of here, I'm going straight to Gary and thanking him for letting you come here. Not many husbands would put up with their wives giving support to a prisoner, much less a guy from high school days."

"Well, Gary wasn't happy with the idea of me coming here, but he didn't try to stop me. He knows we are just friends," Shannon said. She didn't want to be reminded of Gary. She quickly shifted the subject.

"So, tell me what it's like in here."

"Ah, Red, this is not a pretty place." Tony lowered his voice and motioned for Shannon to come closer so she could hear him. "Most of the guys here have done some hard time. A few of them, like me, were framed for crimes they didn't commit. I mostly keep my head down and my ears open and just get through each day. There's a lot of bullies here, pieces of crap who try to rule the world from within. It's hard to trust anyone here, because they can turn on you in an instant."

"I hope you're being careful."

"I am, Red. The Marines spent a lot of time training me for combat. Of course, my military accomplishments don't count for anything around here, but I can hold my own when it comes to defending myself against the punks. Now, let's talk about something pleasant. Tell me about you. What have you been up to lately? And how's that sassy friend of yours, Marie?"

For the next two hours, they reminisced and talked about their high school days. Shannon told him about her boys and shared pictures from her wallet. It was hard to talk over the din of all the conversations flowing around them but the occasional silence between them was comfortable.

"I can't imagine the hell you're going through here," Shannon said.

"I know there's an end to this–that's what keeps me going. I've been fortunate to have a friend or two here. They watch my back and I watch theirs. This is not an easy place, that's for sure."

All too soon, their time was up and Tony walked her back toward the guard desk. "Red, I've got a package for you. You can pick it up from the guard station where you came in. I want to thank you, girl. You coming here means so much to me." He grabbed her in a long hug. As they broke apart, he leaned over and kissed her.

The kiss was quick, but it wasn't a simple peck on the cheek–it was a full on, lip-to-lip kiss. Shannon stood there in shock. She wasn't expecting a kiss like that.

"Bye, Red."

Before she could say anything, he turned and walked toward the back of the room. Back into the cells.

Shannon stood there for another minute, then walked back to the guard desk to pick up her license. She made her way back through the double doors and stopped to pick up the package waiting for her. It was a book and an envelope.

Back in the car, Shannon gingerly opened the envelope and pulled out a sheet of red paper. The familiar scrawl of Tony's handwriting filled one side of the page.

Red, thank you for today. You'll never know how much it means to me. You are the best present I've ever received in this place. Enclosed is a present for you, one of my favorite books. I would much rather it be something bright and sparkly (those days will come) but for now, it's the best I can do. The Shack is a book which made me cry, but I learned something really profound from it–I learned my faith in God is rock solid and my path here on earth is just a temporary one. Everything happens for a reason and I believe my journey in this prison is a test of my faith. I just have to stay strong through it and I know I'll come out of here a better man. I know you're on your own path of finding your faith again and I hope The Shack gives you the insight you're looking for. Always remember, there's another Book which will guide you. Look for the wisdom and guidance you need in that Book.

Thank you for your love and friendship–it means the world to me. YOU are my world right now. My best to you and your family.

Hugs,

Tony

"So how did it go?" Cathy asked when Shannon stepped into the house. She put her purse down on the table and sank back into the kitchen chair. She closed her eyes and rubbed her forehead.

"Well, he looks really different. He's really aged," said Shannon. "He's put on some weight and has some gray in his hair, but he's the same old Tony that I remember. He's got the same intense blue eyes."

"What did you guys talk about? What's it like at the prison?"

"It was awkward at first, but we quickly slipped into our old, comfortable friendship. He told me more in depth about the circumstances that landed him there. Cathy, by the end of the second hour, I had no doubt that he's innocent. He's in there because he was framed. He was beaten so horribly when he was in jail that he simply had nothing left when they offered him a plea agreement."

Cathy shrugged. "Well, it's just hard to believe that he's doing ten years of prison because of something he supposedly didn't do. Like I've always told you, just be careful. I don't want to see you getting tangled up too much in this. I know you want to support him, but just remember, Gary and the kids need you. You have to stay focused on your family."

"I know. Thanks for letting me stay here. Let's grab some lunch and then I'll head home."

When Shannon walked into the house, she found a note on the kitchen table. "We are at the movies. Picking up a pizza on the way home."

Shannon sat on the couch and reflected on her visit with Tony. The kiss was so foreign to her. It had been awhile since Gary had even kissed her. The feeling of Tony's lips upon hers left her with a thrill of excitement. Shannon thought back to the high school years and the kiss on the cliff. She realized the same feelings were floating back up again–the feelings of confusion mixed with joy. Friendship mixed with love.

Or was it lust?

Was she crazy to even feel something again?

Shannon had to do something with all the nervous energy she was feeling at the moment. She put on some music and tackled the dishes in the sink. By the time Gary and the boys arrived home, Shannon was scrubbing the grout between the kitchen tiles.

"What are you doing?" Gary stared at her. He had never seen her scrub grout before.

"Oh, I just got sidetracked while washing the dishes and noticed how grungy the grout had become. I figured I would tackle it."

"Hey mom, we picked up pizza! We got your favorite, garlic veggie." Zach opened up the box to reveal a spinach and tomato pizza.

Shannon wasn't hungry, but she forced down a slice of pizza while she listened to the boys chatter about the afternoon movie. Gary was quiet. He was scrolling through his phone in between bites. The boys took off to their rooms as Shannon cleared the table.

"So how was the prison?"

Shannon shrugged. "There's not much to tell. Tony and I mostly talked about the old days and he told me a little more of how he ended up in prison. He was definitely framed. It's pretty sad what those cops did to him when he was first arrested. They beat him up horribly."

"Look, Shannon, I trust your judgment, but be careful what you believe. There's two sides to every story out there and I'm just saying he might be telling you a version that's different from what actually happened."

"I get it, Gary. I'm not going into this with my eyes closed. I'm just providing some support."

"All right. I'm outta here for a while. I've got a few work emails to catch up on." Gary grabbed his phone and headed into the office.

It was going to be another lonely night.

A few days later, another letter from Tony arrived.

Red,

Your visit was amazing! Girl, you smelled so good and I just wanted to hug you for the longest time. It's been so long since I saw you and all the old memories came flooding back. I'm so, so sorry about the kiss goodbye—I really meant to kiss you on the cheek but I couldn't help myself and the kiss just landed on your lips. But still, it's a kiss in friendship and nothing for your hubby to get upset about. I sure hope I didn't upset you. You look absolutely fantastic and just the way I remembered you in high school, except even better!

I hit a low funk after you left. Your visit was such a high for me that the low after you left just surprised me. I haven't had many visitors to this place, so you coming to see me did something to my heart I haven't felt in a long time. I've blocked out so much. It's easier to survive when you don't feel anything.

Seeing you again brought back a lot of memories from high school. Those years were such a carefree time in our lives. Our friendship was so deep back then, even though I had only known you for a few years. You were the girl I could open up my craziest thoughts to and bounce ideas off of—and I knew you'd never laugh at me. You and I shared a love of horses that no one else could understand. I don't think I've ever had a friendship like that, not even with my closest guy friends. You're unique, Red. You're special. And I thank you for the gift of your friendship–it means a lot to me.

Now about your sons, go easy on them, they're just testing the boundaries with you. That's what all teenagers do. They're both the same age and they probably think alike, so the challenge is two-fold for you. I can remember testing my parents all through high school. Whenever they would set a boundary for me, I would do everything I could to break it, just because I could. I got in a lot of trouble for that. Every time they tried to control me, I rebelled. I know I turned my mom's hair gray at a young age!

What are your plans for Thanksgiving? Will you be doing any cooking? I'm actually looking forward to the Thanksgiving meal here because the food is always a tad better on the holidays. Instead of instant potatoes, they throw in the real stuff. What's your favorite drink? What's your favorite wine? I'm somewhat of a wine snob. I like the good stuff. I took some wine classes over the years and I'm partial to the dry wines. Give me a Merlot any day! I don't like anything sweet. Beer is not my thing either. I'm not much of a drinker– if you remember from high school days, my father was an alcoholic. I never wanted to go down that road so I was always careful about drinking.

Anyway, I was thinking about our visit and it still amazes me that you recognized me so easily across the room. When I look in the mirror, I certainly don't see the person I used to be. Sometimes I don't recognize myself, but a lot of that has to do with the depressing place I'm in. I'm not vain enough any longer to worry about the gray hair. I've earned it. I'm working on getting the old "six-pack" back so I've been hitting the weights lately.

How did it go when you arrived home? Was the hubby upset about you coming to see me? I don't blame him, but I'm glad that you came. I won't forget that you did. Thanks for sharing the pictures of your family. Your boys are strapping young men. I can see a lot of you in them. You've raised them well.

Red, I'm always trying to look at the bright side of things and I've learned a lot about myself during my time here. I'm not the same guy I was before. I'm learning each day to be better than the day before. Just bear with me as I go through this journey. I promise to be a forever friend to you.

I've also learned that you can't make someone love you, all you can do is be someone who can be loved. Families aren't biological either. I'm so glad you're part of mine. It's not what you have in your life, it's who you have in it that matters! Thank you for being in my life. Sending you lots of love.

Hugs,

Tony

15.

The tension between Shannon and Gary was escalating. Gary was coming home later and later each night. He was wearing new clothes--expensive, Italian-made shirts and leather shoes.

"Why are you staying out so late each night?"

"Sorry--we've got some new clients and they require a lot of time."

"Until eleven at night? Who the hell has clients late at night?"

"I've got a lot of reports and prep work. It's only temporary. Things should go back to normal in a few weeks when the project moves along."

"Do you think what's going on between us is normal?"

"What do you mean?"

"We hardly seem to be having a relationship, much less a marriage lately. We haven't had dinner together in many nights and I'm alone more than I'm with you. You're wearing a lot of new clothes. Are you seeing someone?"

"Look, I'm working hard to keep the good life for us. We've got this house and nice cars. It takes me a lot of hours to make the money that I do. My job requires networking with a constant stream of new people and I just want to look my best."

"You seem to forget that I work too."

"I can't help it if my work requires lots of hours lately. You'll need to just deal with it. It's late, I gotta get to bed. I have a lot of new clients I have to take care of tomorrow. We'll talk about it some other time." He switched off the light.

Shannon couldn't sleep. She got out of bed and sat in the darkened kitchen. The blue shimmer from the refrigerator light cast a soft glow around the room. Shannon turned on the kitchen light and pulled out her writing pad.

Dear Tony,

It was really good to see you. I do wish our circumstances were different. It pains me to know that you're in that environment day in and day out. I look forward to the day you get out. With all the changes you've made in your life while in that place–I have no doubt you'll have a good life once again when you're out of there.

Gary was strangely indifferent about our visit. He didn't really ask me any questions. He's been acting weird lately--sometimes I wonder if he's seeing someone. He comes home later and later. This is unusual for a guy who used to be in bed by nine p.m. every night. But then again, he is quite driven and has always been competitive about his sales numbers at work. When he sets goals, he becomes hyper-focused on achieving them. Maybe I'm just over-reacting to all of this.

I have to admit, your kiss really threw me off, but not as bad as the first one did in high school. I think it's because I've been so lonely in my marriage that it felt good to have some human contact again. I am sitting here looking back and realizing that I can't even remember the last time Gary kissed me with any feeling. He still gives me a kiss every now and then in front of the boys–but I think it's out of habit. The romance between us has definitely died out. We are arguing more and more lately. I am really starting to wonder if there's anything left in my marriage.

On a more positive note, in less than a year, you'll be out and free again! What's the first thing you want to do when you get out? I know you probably want a steak dinner! And here's another thought–we should saddle up and go on a ride. We can use the horses from the place I volunteer at. It would really be fun and I know a wonderful trail that's similar to the one we went on in high school. Wow, a lot of memories are really flooding back. I remember the picnic we had at the creek–it was the last picnic before you went off to the Marines. We had some really deep conversations

*that day–about life, our futures, our biggest regrets...
I remember telling you that my biggest regret would
be to get to the end of my life feeling like I never lived
it fully. Well, I'm sitting here feeling like I never lived
it fully–I settled for the safe job, the safe marriage,
and the safe lifestyle. I'm looking back and realizing
that I've lost myself along the way. The stuff that
Gary and I fight about is incredibly silly and I'm now
realizing it's because I've been so checked out on my
own life that I've lost myself in it all.*

Here's to finding myself again!

*Since the boys have a full schedule for the next two
months, I won't be able to head out to see you for a
while, but I'm looking forward to the next visit!*

Love,

Shannon

Shannon sealed the envelope and put it in her purse.
She walked over to the family room, plopped down
on the couch, and turned on the TV. She just wanted
a trashy romance movie to take her mind off of
her home situation. She settled for an old classic,
"Beaches." It wasn't long and she was bawling at the
ending. Shannon turned off the TV and fell asleep on
the couch. She had a long day at the therapeutic center
coming up and a tough week at work. Her boss was
moving out of state and a new one was coming in

from another department.

Hey Red, sounds like you're incredibly busy lately. I hope you get some down time soon. Sorry to hear that you've got a dark cloud situation going on at home. Hang in there and do your best—that's all you can do. Most arguments are silly in retrospect but sometimes they are necessary to clear the air. You can't help what you feel. You can only control how you react to the feelings. Emotions are a tough thing to rein in sometimes! I see that a lot in prison. Every single day, fights break out around here. I do my best to keep my head down and stay out of things. Some of the fights are pretty brutal. The guards are slow to respond because we are considered the scum of the earth here. Not long after I came here, I witnessed my first death. One of the inmates choked another guy to death. The guards were nowhere to be found until it was too late. No one stepped in to stop it because there's a lot of fear if you intervene. I had a terrible time falling asleep that night.

Just eleven more months until I get out of this hell hole. The heat is miserable in here again. The heat index hit 111 yesterday. I had a migraine so bad the other day I could barely lift my head off the bunk. And as you can imagine, it's no fun being in the same room with a toilet. They don't even bother cleaning this place so the stench is pretty bad at times. I try not to dwell on the number of days left since each day is so long. The minutes tick by like hours and hours. What keeps me going is the thought of being able to get on a horse again and hit the trails with you. Too bad my uncle sold the ranch. Those were good times in the past and I would love to revisit them again, minus the kissing of course. That's strictly off limits now that you're a taken woman. (wink)

Father's Day was a hard one this year. I got up early–I couldn't sleep. Took out the few pictures I have of my kids and just sat there and cried. I brought up some good memories and tried to focus on those. Earlier in the week, I wrote a long letter to the kids and sent that off. That's another letter that will go unanswered, I'm sure. At least it is cathartic for me to write to them. I just hope that someday they will wake up and realize they still have a father, despite my many flaws. I love my kids so much that sometimes the hurt is unbearable.

I spoke with a case worker from the prisoner benefit program and she was quite attractive and very nice. She wanted to know all about me--my past, my education, my work experience, and my skills. She seemed quite amazed at what I shared. So, of course, the inevitable question came up and she wanted to know how I ended up in here. I spilled the story and she didn't even bat an eye.

"The same thing happened to my brother but he was able to beat his case," she told me.

Of course, for one quick moment, I was filled with

regret for signing that plea agreement and I often wonder what would have happened if I had not signed it, but I have to put it out of my mind. What's done is done.

But guess what, I've got some good news, I found out I am eligible for funding to get a Masters degree. So back to school I go when I get out of here! This news helps the time to go by quicker! I'm going to study Theology and devote the rest of my life to God and helping others. I got a little slice of hope from this case worker. She treated me like a human being instead of just another number in a prison uniform. That's a precious commodity these days. The only other place I get it from is you, girl. Thank you for being there and seeing past the ugliness that brought me here.

I love you,

Tony

The door opened and Gary walked in the kitchen. He had a scowl on his face. Shannon was sure it was from another bad day at work. He threw his briefcase on the counter and loosened his tie. He glanced at the letter on the counter.

"I see your boyfriend wrote to you again."

Shannon didn't say anything. She quietly folded the

letter and put it back in the envelope. The tension between the two of them had escalated over the last few weeks. They bickered over the smallest things; the glass he left on the coffee table, the new purse she bought last week. They no longer spent any time together in bed. They had drifted apart in more ways than one.

Gary was not around most weekends–he was playing more and more golf with his colleagues. Shannon thought it was strange, as Gary never liked playing during the hotter months. He was missing more and more of the twins' activities and Shannon was feeling like a single parent.

"Lots of new clients coming in," he told her. "I'm doing this for work, not for me. Besides, the new bonus I received will go toward the boys' college funds."

"Well, is there any way you can cut back? It doesn't seem like our checking account is reflecting all the hours you're putting in. You're never here for the boys anymore."

"That's because I put the money in the boys' account– that's why. What are you talking about? You've been spending some of your weekends in prison."

"Gary, I've only gone once. If it bothers you that much, I can stop. I can stop with the letters too."

"No, I didn't mean to jump on you, but you have to realize my time is spent working. The house, the cars, the trips–our lifestyle–it all comes at a cost. I have to hustle out there to keep it all going."

"I really don't care about all that," Shannon retorted. "If you want, we can sell the house and live in a trailer. I'd be perfectly fine with that arrangement. There's a hell of a lot more to life than all the stuff you collect. And by the way, I work too!"

Gary didn't respond. He removed his tie and threw it on the chair. Without saying a word, he grabbed a bag of pretzels and a beer and went into his office.

Screw this, Shannon thought. She grabbed the empty pan off the stove and shoved it into the cabinet. She was not going to cook tonight. Instead, she grabbed the keys and headed out to her car. She just wanted to get away. Anywhere. Somewhere she could think. The boys weren't going to be home until after eight. She glanced at the clock. She had two hours.

Shannon drove to The Coffee Klatch, a local coffee shop that was part-bookstore and part-cafe. She brought a spiral-bound notebook and pen with her.

"Double espresso and a spinach wrap, please."

The shop was bustling with customers, but Shannon found an empty couch in the corner. Halfway through her sandwich, she began to write. At first, she poured out all of her frustrations on a page. Then she flipped the notebook open to a clean page and started over.

> *Tony,*
>
> *Well, the dark cloud situation is even darker. Gary*

and I simply can't get along lately. There are some days I just want to walk away from all of this and just be on my own. I can't do that to the boys, though. They would be devastated. I honestly don't know if I love Gary anymore–I've forgotten that feeling I had in our early days of being in love. We've grown so far apart that there isn't much holding us together. He works so much lately that we hardly see him. Sometimes I wonder if there's another woman, but I don't think so as he has been golfing a lot with his buddies and clients at work and he probably loves his job more than he even loves me.

When I get into these moods, I have to stop and remind myself to be grateful for all that I have because I have my freedom, something that you're paying a price for. It puts a lot of things in perspective and gives me a good reason to look at my life with totally different eyes.

Work has been crazy hectic lately. I have a new boss who came over from another department and she's such a micromanager that I dread going to work now. She picks apart all of my reports and sometimes she comes in when I'm working with a patient and she will actually tell me how she wants me to do my job. I've been at this hospital forever–no one has ever been hurt or died on my shift–and I don't think I can take her management style for the long term. For now, I just bite my lip and do what she wants me to do.

Well, enough of the negative stuff. Let's talk about

something happy–like the fact that your days are getting closer and closer to freedom. I'm heading to the bookstore soon to get something new to read. I'll keep an eye out on books that I can order for you. Is there a book of some kind that you've always wanted to read? Or do you want me to surprise you with one of my favorites? I'm currently reading a Danielle Steel novel. I'm guessing that won't be up your alley. Let me know what book you'd like and I'll send one off to you.

Love, Red

The tension between Shannon and Gary continued to escalate. They could no longer hide their troubles from the boys.

"What's with Dad?" Zach asked. "He's been missing a lot of our games."

"He's just been working with a lot of new clients," Shannon said.

"Well, he always manages to find time to go golfing with clients–why can't he find time to be with us?"

"He's just been under a lot of stress lately trying to get everything done. I think once he gets settled in with the new clients, he will have more time at that point."

Shannon really didn't want to cover up for Gary but she also didn't want the boys to stress out over the obvious chasm that was developing between the two of them. Gary was still kissing her here and there, but his mind seemed to be elsewhere whenever they spent time together.

16.

"Shannon, can you meet me at the new sandwich shop on Bachman street?"

Shannon glanced at the clock, it was only 10:30 in the morning.

"What's up, Marie? You never call this early on a Sunday."

"I just got in late yesterday evening and there's something I want to talk to you about."

"Can't you just tell me over the phone?"

"Shannon, I haven't seen you in a while and I wanted to catch up. Just meet me there in an hour. Besides, you need to eat, too."

As they dug into their breakfast sandwiches, the two of them caught up with each other. Halfway through the meal, Marie put down her sandwich.

"Shannon, I have to tell you something. I'm not sure the best way to tell you this except straight out. On my way home from the airport yesterday, I stopped to have a late dinner with my crew at a restaurant downtown. I saw Gary there...with a woman."

"Oh?"

"At first, I didn't think much of it, but then I realized it was a Saturday night and it couldn't possibly be a client. Then I saw him reach over and grab her hand. He was really affectionate. He pushed a purple box across the table and she opened it. It was a necklace and as far as I could see, it was a diamond encrusted necklace."

Shannon gasped. "Gary gave me a diamond necklace when we first started getting serious."

"It gets worse. I kind of snuck out after they left and they were kissing pretty deeply while waiting for the valet. She got into a black Mercedes and took off. What time did Gary get home last night?"

"He came in around 11:30 last night and went straight to bed. He told me he was playing poker with a couple of guys from work."

"Has he ever stayed out overnight?"

"He was gone last weekend for a work retreat. He said it was the first one that the company had set up."

"He's cheating on you."

"That would explain a lot. We've grown so far apart lately. He's been wearing nicer clothes. He came home with new leather boots the other day–he hasn't worn boots in years. I just thought it was because he was trying to move up at work. He mentioned a new woman at work–her name is...I'm trying to remember it... yeah, Donna. What does she look like?"

"Well, he's obviously getting close to whoever this gal is. She's a classy gal–Gucci, Chanel–high heels, and a $600 belt. Long, dark hair and a nice rack. No married guy spends an innocent Saturday night with a gal, just saying."

"Six hundred dollar belt?" Shannon raised her eyebrows.

"I have the same belt at home. Don't deflect the subject, girl."

Shannon sat there in silence.

"What are you going to do?"

"How the hell do I know? I just found out my husband's probably cheating on me–or is about to. Looking back on the last few months, it all makes sense now. All those new, expensive clothes. For years, I could never get him in a shopping mall and I bought most of his clothes. I just thought he was finally shopping for himself lately because of his promotion."

"You need to dump the shit head."

"Marie, I need time to think. My world just went upside down."

Dear Tony,

Well, I have some interesting news here. Seems like my biggest fears about Gary having an affair are true. Marie saw him having dinner with a woman one Saturday night. After I confronted Gary, he confessed to everything. Turns out it wasn't just one woman, he had been seeing someone else a year before this! He broke down crying, saying he didn't want to hurt me or the boys. I knew in my heart that my marriage was over. There was no saving this. He begged for counseling. I agreed to go, only for us to figure out ways to do the divorce and not hurt the boys in the process. He thinks there's a sliver of hope that we can repair this.

Right after this happened, I sat down and had a good, hard look at my marriage throughout the years and tried to imagine a future with Gary. I couldn't see one. We had drifted so far apart that I came to realize it was the boys holding us together. I had filled my life up with so many other things that I didn't need nor want Gary in my future. I'm going to navigate life ahead with this new sense of 'self' and see where the journey takes me.

I went to see Marie's lawyer and liked him immediately. He took care of two divorces with Marie. I served Gary with divorce papers pretty quickly and he moved out that day. We both agreed to divide things up in a fair way. There isn't much that I want except to stay in the house and keep things stable for the boys. In our first counseling session, the therapist was really helpful in guiding us. I was able to connect with some of my anger and get it out. Gary just listened, for once. After two years of deceit and being with two other women, there was no way that I could love him again.

I dread what this is going to do to my boys once it is final, but there's no way around it. I'm glad they are teenagers and not young children–somehow I think that's easier. The boys are angry at Gary and refuse to spend much time with him. He doesn't seem to understand their anger. I think he's actually so relieved to have the freedom to be with this new woman that he doesn't want to deal with the fallout from this.

I am just a jumbled mess here. I feel so incredibly betrayed by Gary because of how long this was going on. I'm doing my best to hold myself together, but I find myself crying a lot in the bathroom at work. I always thought we would be the kind of couple that would celebrate 50 years of marriage. I'm just really sad right now and I can't figure out what my next steps are going to be for myself.

Marie has been a great source of support and she checks on me daily. If it wasn't for her, I think I wouldn't be able to function each day. She calls me in the morning and gives me a pep talk for the day. She's been through two divorces so she's a veteran at that. Sometimes she can be so silly, but her wry humor takes the edge off the hurt. She's already hunting for

ANNE VALLE

a guy for me to date–can you believe that? She tells me I just need a rebound guy to have some fun with and not get serious at all. I'm just not ready to even go there. This is all raw and real and sometimes I just feel like I'm in a dream and I'll wake up and life will be like it was.

Well, let's change the subject and talk about something happy–which is your release day! Three more months and you'll be tasting freedom again! I'm going to take you out to dinner and we shall celebrate with some nice wine and a big steak. No more rice and beans for you! I know just the place to take you, so we shall eat well and celebrate.

I'm going to come in to see you next weekend–looking forward to seeing you again!

Love,

Shannon

As soon as her shift ended on Friday, Shannon drove out to her sister's house. Cindy met her at the door with a hug.

"I'm sorry you're going through this, sis. What do you plan to do?"

"Well, I'm going to try to keep everything stable for the boys while we go through this. I'm so angry at Gary for messing up our family life. The boys don't deserve this."

"Hon, the boys deserve a happily married mom and dad–they weren't getting that. You've been miserable with Gary for years."

"What do you mean?"

"Over the last few years, I've seen you becoming more withdrawn and sad–and the fights you've had have escalated. Come in, I've got something to show you."

On the kitchen table, Cindy had several photo albums. Shannon was shocked to see the progression from happiness to sadness as they scrolled through the years of photos. Cindy had caught many pensive moments between Shannon and Gary in the recent years at family gatherings. As the years went on, there were less and less pictures of the two of them together.

"Gosh, I feel like I was just oblivious to my marriage falling apart but seeing these photos really puts it all together. I've been hanging on by a thread for a while now."

"Well, now it's time to take care of yourself. What time are you heading out to see Tony? I made us some lunch. I figured we could eat before you go."

"Yeah, I'm hungry! I'll head out at two–it's less crowded by that point and most of the crying toddlers are gone by then."

"Hey, you look beautiful!" Tony wrapped his arms around her in a long hug. "I'm so happy to see you. My whole world just lights up when I can see you face to face. And this time, you're on your way to being a free woman!"

Shannon sat down with a wry smile. "It's a turn of events I certainly didn't expect. I'm not sure how I feel about it anymore, but it is what it is. I'm slowly coming to terms with it."

"Shannon, if there's one thing I've learned about being caught in a situation that you cannot change–it is this: the sooner you roll with it, the less energy you expend trying to change it. Now, I know you're not in a prison like me, but one of the worst prisons is in your mind–and you have the ability to free that."

"How are you so wise?" she laughed.

"I learned it the hard way," he grinned.

Shannon stayed for two hours and they talked non-stop. Their conversation was filled with laughter as they shared stories of adventures they experienced throughout the years.

"What's an adventure you want to experience when you get out of here?" Shannon asked.

"I want to rent a catamaran with a private captain for

a day and sail away. I want to see a brilliant sunset before we head back to shore and call it a day."

"That sounds like fun. Why don't we do that to celebrate once you get out of here?"

"Would you really do that, Shannon?"

"Well, yeah. Remember, I'm not going to be married anymore at some point. It's time for me to have some fun, too. I've been working so hard for so long and now it's my turn. And as long as you can promise me that we will return to shore in one piece, let's do it!"

"Well, I can't promise that we won't be eaten by sharks when we snorkel, but I'll do my best to save you," he laughed.

"You know, I can't wait for you to get out. It's been so good to have our friendship back. It feels like we picked up right where we left off in high school."

Tony gave her a long, warm hug. Minus a kiss. "See you again, Red. I love you for everything you've done for me and for everything our friendship has been. You are the reason I'm able to get through each day here."

17.

The bang of the judge's gavel made it all real. The dissolution of their marriage was final.

"I should feel something, but I feel nothing," Shannon told Marie.

"It's okay, babe, it's a new beginning. You're just closing the door on your marriage, but another one is opening up." Marie put her arm around Shannon. "I've done this twice. You gotta give yourself time to adjust to all this new stuff. Plus, you can open up your new account on Tinder and learn how to swipe."

Shannon laughed.

"I am definitely not dating again. I have sworn off men! I never want to open up my heart and get hurt again."

"You never know, girl. Your Prince Charming might be just a swipe away."

The absence of a band of steel on her left hand felt strange to Shannon. She sold her diamond ring and went on a shopping spree with Marie, buying all new clothes and shoes. Shannon went through her closet and gave away bags and bags of clothes with memories tied to Gary. The dress she wore to one of Gary's work events–gone. The fancy coat he bought her with one of his bonuses–gone. The leather boots he gave her one Christmas–gone.

"How's the new wheels?"

"Ah, I love the new convertible. Of course, I kept the van, too, for the boys, but the new car is all mine! Gary had to fork over half his retirement and cash, so I figured I was going to get myself a present for all the crap he put me through. I also get a massage once a week and I've added pedicures to my manicure routine."

"Well, girl, you deserve it. You pretty much ran the house and did all the cooking and cleaning all these years–while working, too. I'm glad you're taking care of yourself." Marie reached over and gave Shannon a long hug.

The months flew by as Shannon and the boys adjusted to their new normal. When the boys were with Gary, Shannon visited Tony. Marie was not pleased, she felt that Shannon was spending far too much time with Tony.

"Honestly, I don't trust him," she said one night. "I'm still not convinced he is innocent and I would hate to see you get in deep with him and get hurt in the process."

"Look, I love you my friend, but with this one, you have to trust my own judgment. I'm a big girl. I know I just got divorced, but I'm not going to jump into another relationship. I have a friendship with Tony that runs really deep, but it's just that–a friendship. He's supportive and really listens when I'm down and struggling. Whether or not it turns into something else, I don't know if we'll ever go down that path. Right now, I'm going to enjoy his company, his conversations, and his 'love' for me as a friend. So please, just back off on this and give me some space to be me on this journey."

Marie sighed. "Ok, girl. I won't bring it up again. I just want you not to get hurt again. That's all. You know I love you, too." Marie held out her arms and wrapped Shannon in a hug.

"Come on, let's go have a good lunch with a couple of cocktails and celebrate this new path of yours."

Shannon pulled up to the prison parking lot and parked the convertible. This would be the last time she would have to drive here. Today, Tony was walking out a free man.

This time, she didn't have to go inside for a pat down. She waited outside the door. She glanced at her watch. It was taking longer than she thought it would. Shannon paced back and forth. The temperature was rising with every passing minute.

The door finally swung open.

"Hey Red!" Tony had a small bag and came bounding over to her. "This is probably one of the happiest days of my life! Thank you for being here! He kissed her on the cheek and enveloped her in a tight hug. "I can't wait to see those new wheels. Lead me there!"

Shannon drove Tony to the "halfway" house where he would be staying for six months. She stayed in the car as he went in. He signed in and went through the orientation process. Forty five minutes later, Tony dropped off his bag in his room and headed back outside.

"How's the place?" Shannon asked.

"It's not quite paradise, but it's a hell of a lot better than prison, I can tell you that! Now, where are we going for that sumptuous dinner?"

"I made a reservation at my favorite steak house," Shannon said. "The steaks are like butter there–in fact, you can cut them with a butter knife. But first, why don't we head over to the mall and get you some new clothes and a few things for your room."

"Red, I don't have a lot of money just yet and I really don't want you spending money on me. The dinner is enough. I don't know if I can even secure a job with my past. There's a lot of unknowns at this point."

"Tony, look, right now, I just want to help you out. I know you would do the same thing for me if the situation was reversed. One day, you'll be making money again, but for now, please let me help you get comfortable and settled in."

"All right. It's a bit uncomfortable for me, but I welcome your support."

"That's much better. Now let's go shopping and then hit that steak house."

"You ready, Red?"

Shannon nodded. Tony untied the rope that was holding the catamaran to the pier. With his foot, he pushed the sailboat and nimbly hopped on. The captain started the engine and guided the boat out into the bay. Shannon sat down next to Tony.

"I can't believe we are lucky enough to do this," he said. "There were many times in prison when I dreamed of spending time with you. I don't have many friends who are willing to do adventurous things. I'm glad you were willing to do this with me."

"As long as we don't get too far from shore," she laughed. "I don't want to end up in the middle of the ocean. I would hate for us to be lost at sea!"

"Don't worry, I told the captain and he said he will hug the shore."

Their plan was to sail for a few hours and stop to scuba dive at a popular reef. The sun was hanging high in the sky, with just a few clouds dotted around. The captain stopped the engine. There was no sound except the water hitting the pontoons. He unleashed the sail. There wasn't much of a breeze, but just enough to lazily push the boat against the gentle waves.

"It's just beautiful out here," Shannon said.

"I feel incredibly free," Tony smiled. "Every day in prison was worth this moment right now. It's a great day to enjoy the sun. Come on, let's lie here for a bit."

Shannon plopped down next to him and took off her t-shirt. She was wearing a brand new sapphire-blue swimsuit that showed off her curves.

"Oh girl, you're blinding me–you're more beautiful than anything I remember as a teen–and I'm saying this affectionately as a friend."

"Well, you've got a nice six-pack from all those workouts you've been doing. I'm pretty impressed, myself."

Shannon and Tony laid back against the mesh netting. The occasional salty spray covered them in a fine mist. Two dolphins popped up and swam playfully as the boat sailed along.

A short time later, the captain turned the boat into the wind and the sail wavered back and forth. He released the anchor.

"Ok, you two. Here's where we are going to snorkel. My only rule is to stay within 100 yards or so–don't be swimming off where I can't find you. Stay between the boat and the shore. If you want to swim to the shore, that's fine. This spot is pretty private–only a few other boats anchor here occasionally. I'll give you privacy," he winked, "But I'll still keep an eye on you to be safe."

"Don't worry, we won't be swimming out toward the ocean," Shannon laughed. "I have a healthy fear of being swept off in the current, so I'll be sticking close to shore."

Shannon and Tony explored the reefs as colorful fish darted about. A sea turtle swam lazily along the bottom. Tony pointed out a lionfish and motioned for Shannon to stay away. When they reached the shore, they collapsed in the sand on their backs.

"This is paradise." Tony said. "Freedom never tasted so sweet." He turned on his side to look at Shannon. "Red, if I died tomorrow, this would be the best day of my life."

Shannon looked into his eyes. The same blue eyes she remembered from high school seemed even more blue next to the Caribbean waters. Deep inside, she felt a stirring that was strange, yet so familiar. She leaned over and her lips met Tony's.

This time, the kiss was hers.

Tony slid his hands across her shoulders and pulled her closer. The hunger they felt was from deep within, buried by years of denial.

Tony pulled away. "Red, are you sure about this?"

"Yes, I've never been more sure. It feels right. The right time, wrong place, though." She pointed back at the catamaran. "The captain has eyes."

Tony laughed.

"Red, I want to take this slow. I've always jumped the gun with women and screwed up royally. I don't want to screw this up with you. But I can tell you this, when we get back, I want to court you, date you, woo you, and love you."

Back on the catamaran, they enjoyed dinner as the sun began to sink in the sky. As the catamaran glided across the calm waters, Tony wrapped his arm around Shannon's shoulders, pulling her close. She rested her head against his chest, feeling the steady rhythm of his heartbeat. They watched as the sun began its descent, casting a golden hue over the horizon.

"This is just the beginning, Red. Just the beginning."

18.

The first time they made love, it was slow and sweet. Tony booked a tiny home on a nearby lake. As the sun rose and peeked through the slats, they lay entwined in the sheets. Shannon was happy. The heartache she felt at the end of her marriage was replaced by this new, comforting feeling of the old and new combined into one.

Tony woke up and smiled at her. "You're an early bird, aren't you?"

"I can't help it–it's all those years of getting up and doing long shifts at the hospital."

"Well, I'm going to teach you how to slow down time and savor it."

"I like that."

"And guess what…it's my turn to get up early and go to work, starting Monday."

"You found a job?" Shannon looked at him in surprise.

"Yup!" I called an old buddy of mine and he connected

me with a guy out here who owns the Happy House over on 22nd street. He's going to let me work at the restaurant. It's not much, but it's a start. I'll probably be a prep cook and dishwasher for a while, but I'm gonna be grateful to get a regular paycheck, no matter how small it is. I hope you won't be embarrassed to hang out with me anymore. I'm just a lowly kitchen worker now."

"I don't care about jobs and titles, you know me, Tony. I'm just happy for you. It's a step in the right direction as you figure out this new path in life."

"Well, since I've gotta work in a restaurant, I'm going to get out of bed and cook you some breakfast. I think I still remember how to make bacon and eggs. You stay here in bed and relax. I've got this."

Life settled into a routine. Shannon didn't tell anyone about spending time with Tony. She kept it from Marie, knowing that she wouldn't approve. It was too early to introduce Tony to her boys. Cindy was the only one who knew, and she was cautious but supportive.

Every other week, Tony and Shannon explored new activities together. The first time they saddled up horses, it felt like time reversed and they were back in high school again.

"Red, this brings back so many memories for me. I really miss my uncle and the farm. He and my aunt passed away a few years ago and his only son sold everything. There's no going back to that place, so we'll just have to visit it in our memories."

"Well, we will just have to find new trails and create new memories," Shannon said. "Come on, now it's my turn to show you a trail that I love."

They rode in silence through a dry field to reach the edge of a river. As they came to a clearing, they could hear the sounds of water cascading down. "This may be the only place around that has a mini-waterfall. Behold what I call the Texas Niagara!"

Tony laughed at the sight of a single stream of water pouring over a boulder and landing in the river below.

"You're exaggerating just a tad, Red! But it's a rare find in Texas–any water that moves over rocks is a good thing around here."

"No one ever comes around here. I found this quite by accident several years ago when one of the horses took off for the river on a hot day. Let's stop and rest up a bit here."

They took off their shoes and stuck their feet in the cool water.

"Let's go swimming," Tony suggested. "We can skinny dip and cool off a bit."

"I've never done that before."

"Red, there's a first time for everything and no one should go through life without the pleasure of river water on the naked body!"

Shannon hesitated. "What if someone comes by?"

"How popular is this trail in all the years you've been riding it?"

"Very few people use it."

"Well, there ya go, Red." Tony took off his shirt and stripped down to his underwear. "I'll keep this piece of cloth on if it makes you feel better."

"You know what, Tony..." Shannon took off her shirt and flung her bra to the ground. She wiggled out of her shorts and ran for the river. "Last one in is a sissy!"

Tony grinned and dove in. He took his underwear off and tossed them on the bank.

The months flew by. Shannon felt like she was living two lives–one as the mother of her boys and the other as Tony's girlfriend. On one hand, the excitement of being with Tony fueled her days. On the other hand, Shannon often felt like she was walking on eggshells trying to keep a secret that she wasn't ready to share with others.

"Have you started dating yet?" One of her coworkers asked during a break at work.

"My best friend signed me up on a dating app, but I don't really want to focus on that right now. I'm actually enjoying being single."

"I don't blame you. A good man is hard to find these

days! It seems like the dating apps draw out the unusual ones–and that's saying it nicely."

The phone rang. Shannon smiled when she saw Tony's name pop up. She was sitting at home in her nursing scrubs eating leftover spaghetti and watching a romantic comedy.

"Hi! What's up?"

"Hey Red, how's your week going?"

"Coming off a busy shift, but it was good. How's work going?"

"Well, I'm doing more and more cooking, so I'm keeping myself out of trouble. I heard back from my lawyer–even though I'm a free man now, I cannot see my kids until they are 18. My ex-wife moved to an undisclosed location and I cannot even write to them. She has an iron-clad order of protection cast on me."

"I'm sorry, Tony."

"It's a tough blow, but I've just gotta deal with it. Someday, my kids may seek me out again, and until then, I will just continue to live my life. Hey, here's the reason I called you, are you free this Saturday night? Will the boys be with Gary?"

"Yeah, they will. Why?"

ANNE VALLE

"There's a restaurant that I want to take you to, Soveniques. I've been saving up for this steakhouse and I want to get some proper meat into you."

Shannon laughed. "You know that sounds raunchy, don't you?"

"I promise you, it'll be elegant. Put on a dress and some high heels. Let's live the night up. I'll pick you up at 6:30. We have a reservation for seven."

"Ok, sounds like fun. I could never turn down some good meat. I gotta go here, Marie is calling."

Shannon switched the phone to her other ear. "Hey!"

"Hi! It's been awhile since I've seen you! I'm back home from Paris. I don't know what you've been doing to keep busy, but I need some girl time with you. Does Gary have the boys this weekend?"

"Yeah."

"Ok, great! One of my clients gave me a gift card to the Cheesecake Factory–you know how much we love their cheesecake. Let's hit that place this Saturday night."

"Oh, uh, I have plans for that night."

"What's up that night? Are you dating someone, finally? Tinder finally delivered?"

"Well...not exactly. Um..."

"Shit, don't tell me you're going out with Tony?"

"Well, yeah, he offered to take me out as a, um, thank you...for all the support I gave him. You know. Through the prison."

"What's really going on, Shannon? You know, I can read right through you, even through the phone. Are you two in a relationship?"

"No! You know we are friends. We are spending time together, but for crying out loud, I'm allowed to have a life, you know. I don't have to justify what I do to you."

"Look, I'm sorry, I didn't mean for it to come out like that. I just want you to be careful. He's been in prison for a crime and we don't know if he really pushed his wife down those stairs. We don't know if he had sex with his step-daughter–"

"He wasn't accused of having sex, he was accused of suggesting sex, that's a whole different thing."

"Regardless, you know his reputation in high school– he slept around with anything that moved. I don't want to see you next in line for that. You're too good for him, Shannon. Please be careful. You just got divorced. Don't fall in love with him. That's the last thing you need right now."

"Marie, how many times do we have to go over this? Can you please leave it alone? Can you trust me?"

"It's not you–I just don't trust him. Call it a gut thing. I'm scared for you. That's what's really going on. I'm looking out for you."

Shannon hung up. She had never done that to Marie before. The phone rang again, but Shannon ignored it. A text came through. *Look, I'm sorry. I just care about you and I don't want to see you get hurt so soon after all you've been through.*

Shannon felt caught between two people she loved and she didn't know how to handle it. She grabbed the phone and started texting Marie back.

Look, I love you and I appreciate your concern. I'm just asking you to trust me in that I know how my own journey should unfold. I'm not going to do anything rash and stupid. You know I'm the careful type.

Marie texted back. *You're right. I love you, too.*

Shannon smoothed her dress and looked in the mirror. She held up one necklace after another, trying to decide which one would complement her new dress. She picked up a silver chain with a simple red pendant. Shannon decided to splurge on a bright red dress–a color that she had never worn before. She had her nails done in a shimmering pearl color. She heard Tony's car pull up in the driveway. The car was an older model Prius with a few rust spots, but it was all he could afford on his meager salary.

"Wow, Red, you did it again. Every time I see you, the beauty just keeps compounding!" He leaned over and kissed her. "I'm so excited about taking you to this place. I saved up for a while so that we can have a feast. We are going to enjoy the night!"

The steaks were cooked to perfection and the asparagus had a buttery, garlic drizzle on them. The roasted fingerling potatoes were crispy on the outside and delicately soft on the inside. Tony and Shannon shared a salad and had a couple of glasses of wine.

"Dessert, babe?"

"I'm quite full," Shannon said.

"I'm going to insist on some cheesecake. This place makes a decadent peach cheesecake with a crumble on the top that is amazing."

"How do you know this?"

"Yelp reviews," he laughed. "That's how I found this place. Seems like the cheesecake is the most popular item reviewed."

"Ok, I'll have a couple of bites, but I can't manage more than that."

The waiter put the plate down in front of her and left. Shannon noticed a simple diamond ring next to the cheesecake. Her mouth dropped open and she looked at Tony.

Tony got down on one knee. "Red, before you say anything, let me say this. I know this is probably fast considering it's been just a few months since we've been boyfriend and girlfriend. I know you're not even ready to share this kind of thing with the world. But, having said that, I want to give this to you and ask you to be committed to my heart. You don't have to make a decision about marrying me–I just want you to know how much I love you and that I'm pledging my love to you–and only you. Will you take this ring and be a part of my life, however that looks for you?"

"Tony, I'm completely stunned here, but since you're only asking for a commitment, and not marriage, I can say 'yes.' Please know that I need time–and we have to take it one day at a time. But yes, I commit to us being us. The only thing is, I...I can't wear the ring in front of my family, just yet."

Tony slipped the ring on her finger. The customers began to applaud and Tony kissed her. "It's ok, Red. I understand. My heart is just full in knowing that you and I can keep on taking this journey together. One day we can do it with your family by our side. For now, I'm happy to have us."

On Sunday night, Shannon arrived home and slipped the ring into a sock and hid it in her sock drawer. Despite hiding the ring, Shannon's heart was full. Someday, she was going to marry Tony, but for now, she was content for every minute that they had together.

Tony and Shannon saw each other every other weekend when the boys were with Gary. Shannon slipped the ring into her purse and happily put it on her finger whenever she was with Tony. They went to rodeos together and spent time on the trails with the horses they borrowed from the therapeutic riding center.

"Tony, I want my boys to meet you."

Tony looked at her in surprise. "Are you sure?"

"Yes, I'm sure. I'm so tired of 'hiding' you from my family. The boys have heard about you and they know I've written letters to you for a long time. Now it's time to merge the two lanes of joy. I want the boys to get to know you. As if we are friends, you know what I mean? I want to ease into this."

"Red, I'm honored and humbled that you finally feel comfortable to introduce me to your boys. I feel like I already know so much about them and I can't wait to meet them."

"The boys will be home Saturday afternoon. Why don't you swing by around two. We can hit the pool with the boys and make a casual event out of this. That way it's informal and comfortable. The boys love spending time in the pool and that should ease any awkwardness that might come up."

"I'll be there."

The doorbell rang. "Boys, come and meet Tony." Shannon put the knife down. She was slicing cheese for a charcuterie board. Zach and Brandon followed her to the door.

"Hi Tony–meet my boys. This is Zach and here's

Brandon. The boys shook hands with Tony.

"I've heard a lot about you and it's nice to finally meet you two."

"We've heard about you, too. Mom says you two were best friends in high school."

"We definitely were—the two of us could talk about every topic under the sun–and beyond the moon, too." he laughed. "She was the only friend who was willing to ride horses and go to rodeos, no matter how high the temperature hit in Texas!"

The boys found it easy to talk with Tony and they had a pleasant afternoon at the pool throwing a foam football back and forth.

"You want to stay for dinner?" Zach asked. Shannon looked at him in surprise. She wasn't expecting the boys to become comfortable with Tony so fast. They were sitting around the patio table, devouring the last of the crackers and cheese.

Tony looked at Shannon with a quizzical look.

"Sure, why don't we order some Chinese food."

"We can kick back with a movie," Brandon chimed in. "Tom Hanks has a new movie out."

"Well, you said the magic words, your mom and I love Tom Hanks and every movie he's ever made," said Tony. "I'm game! That is, if it's ok with your mom."

"I could never turn down a Tom Hanks movie,"

Shannon laughed.

Later that night, when she slipped into bed, Shannon reflected on the evening with her boys. She was thrilled that they both settled in comfortably with Tony.

19.

"Let's take a sunset ride tonight," Tony suggested. It was a muggy night and the horses were sweating when they stopped to take a break. "Come here, Red, let's sit a bit." Tony whipped out a blanket and spread it on the grass. They laid side by side, looking up at the blue sky in the break between the trees. Tony reached out and held Shannon's hand in his.

"Life has been amazing with you in it," Tony said. "I'm just feeling really grateful that you came into my life at my darkest moment and that you didn't turn away when you heard my story. I don't know how I can ever thank you for bringing light into my life during a time when I could see none."

"Well, you've been with me through my darkest moment of dealing with Gary's infidelity and the divorce."

"Red, let's get married."

Shannon rolled over and looked at him in surprise.

"Tony, it's too soon. My boys still think of you as just a

friend in my life. I haven't even told them how serious it is between us."

"I know you think this is fast, but I don't want to hide anymore. I hate the fact that you have to hide the ring and our relationship. I love you, Red. I want the world to know that. When do you think the time will come when we can share our joy with others?"

"I need a couple more...months. I just need time. Everything is happening so fast."

"Months are not going to make a difference."

"What do you mean?"

"It doesn't make a difference whether you share me tomorrow or several months later, the outcome is the same. We are together, we are planning a lifetime together, and it's time to share that with others. I'm a free man today. My past is behind me. You don't have a problem with my past, why worry about what others are going to think?"

"I'm not worried about other people. I'm thinking more about my boys and how they'll feel." Shannon was also worried about Marie. She knew her friend would not support the idea of marrying Tony.

"What if we do something crazy...let's choose a breathtaking island, go off and get married–just the two of us–and in your own time, you can choose the moment when I truly become completely a part of your life. I'm willing to wait years for you this way."

"Tony, that is crazy!"

"Exactly! Life is meant to be lived. Love like ours comes once in a lifetime. Let's do the 'crazy' and create a life together in a way that only we can. No one has to know, until you're ready, but meanwhile, we'll make a life around our love. There's a place in Cabo where we can get married on Lover's beach. I've been doing a lot of research. Plus, I've been saving up my meager salary. Just you and me, Red. There's even a little cliff called Pelican Rock where we can jump off to celebrate afterwards! What do you say? Live a bit crazy, for once?"

Shannon's heart started beating faster as she thought about the idea of being Tony's wife. He was her friend as well as her lover.

"And Shannon...we never have to tell anyone. When the time is right, we can do a civil ceremony with your friends and family. No one ever has to know. It's just gonna be our thing."

"Okay." Shannon smiled at Tony. "Oh my gosh, I can't believe I'm saying 'okay,' to this absolutely crazy idea, but I feel like this is something I need to do for me. For once, I'm making a decision that's right for me."

"Red, babe, I love you. I love that you're willing to dive off a cliff with me in life. Hey, that would be an awesome adventure after our vows–we can jump off the cliff together!"

"Again, that's crazy, but we'll see. Only if it's a short cliff!"

"You want more 'crazy?' Let's do it in three weeks. I'll book us a nice hotel and we'll head to that beach. Shorts and a nice shirt for me–a beautiful white sundress for you. We will find a local person to marry us and write our own vows. There's an amazing restaurant where we can have our wedding dinner–can you tell I've spent hours dreaming about this and looking up places?"

"I'll need to go shopping!" Shannon laughed. "I cannot believe we are going to do this."

"This is just the start, girl. We have a lifetime of fun ahead."

"There's only one problem–I'll be at a nursing conference in New Orleans until that Friday."

"That's ok, you can fly and meet me down there. I'll need to go down a few days early anyway, to get things ready for us. Meet me there, and we'll have the time of our lives."

"So we're really doing this?"

"We're really doing this, Red. I'm so happy. I love you."

20.

Shannon arrived at the Louis Armstrong airport early in the morning. Her wedding dress was packed–a white, linen sundress with spaghetti straps. Shannon splurged on a pair of white Jimmy Choo flip flops to complete her outfit. She packed her mother's pearl necklace to have "something borrowed." For her hair, she bought a pale blue shell clip.

"I've got a conference to go to in New Orleans and then I'm going to stay a few days to explore the area," she told Gary and the boys. She told Cindy and Marie the same thing."

"You want me to fly down and hang with you," Marie suggested when they met up for coffee earlier in the week. "I've got so many travel points to use up."

"No! I mean, no, sorry–didn't mean to jump with that no–I've got a couple of co-workers who are coming with me. I'm just going to be so busy with the conference and dinners with the co-workers. We are planning to do some sight-seeing."

Shannon felt the guilt creep up. She ignored the feelings and kept a light smile on her face. "It's time for me to have some adventures, you know. This is one of them."

The nursing conference was a wonderful distraction for Shannon as she met up with her coworkers and several working friends. There was almost no time to think as they went from one activity to another.

"You want to ride to the airport with us?" one of her co-workers asked. "What time is your flight?"

"I'm leaving at 4:30."

"You're not on the 2 o'clock flight with us?"

"No, I'm taking a detour and meeting up with a friend."

"Oh, a guy?"

Shannon let out a nervous laugh. "A friend I've known from high school. Just going to have some fun kicking back for a few days."

"That's good, you deserve it. You work hard and it's good that you're going to unwind a bit. Ok, the Uber will be here soon. Meet you in the lobby."

Shannon was thankful that she didn't have to explain more.

"Ma'am is this seat taken?" Shannon looked up. A plump, matronly woman was pointing to the seat next to her. Shannon moved her purse.

"Here. It's all yours now."

After a long wait to get through the screening process, Shannon was finally at the gate and waiting to pass the time. Shannon glanced at her phone. It was another hour before boarding. She reached into her bag and pulled out a novel. She couldn't keep her mind on the story.

Was she doing the right thing? Was she moving too fast with Tony?

Shannon closed her eyes and tried to imagine life after the wedding. She would have to slowly bring Tony into her life more and more, but first, she had to absolutely make sure that they boys would be okay having their relationship move to a more serious level.

Oh my gosh, maybe I shouldn't be doing this. What if the boys get upset about having Tony in their life in a serious way? What if Marie never accepts Tony?

Shannon's feelings were a jumbled mess.

Wait a minute. I love him. I deserve to be loved. It's my life! My happiness matters, too.

Her phone chimed. A text appeared from Marie.

Shannon, call me asap!

Shannon hit the dial in a panic. Did something happen to the boys? Gary?

"What's wrong? Is everything okay? Is someone hurt?"

"I need to talk to you. Where are you now?"

"I'm in New Orleans."

"Sounds like you're in a crowded place. Can you go somewhere quieter? I really have to talk to you."

Shannon glanced around. There really was no "quiet" place at the airport.

"The gate for flight 356 to Cabo San Lucas has been changed–please proceed to gate B12 for this flight."

"Shannon, are you at the airport? Are you coming home?"

"Yeah, I'm at the airport. No, um, I'm not coming home. My co-workers decided on a last minute flight to somewhere fun so we are taking off in about an hour."

"Where are you going?"

"We are going to, um, Cabo. Look, it's none of your business what I'm doing."

"Shannon, are you with Tony?"

"No."

At least that was the truth.

"Ok, look, you're going to absolutely hate me after I share what I have to share. But you gotta know this–I'm your best friend and I love you. It has to do with Tony. He's not innocent."

"What do you mean?"

"Now, don't get mad at me. I hired a private investigator. She is one of the best investigators and she dug up a lot on Tony, including evidence."

"What kind of evidence?"

"Look, first of all, those charges with his step-daughter–well, it's all true, except it's worse than what he told you. He did have sex with her, he forced her, and she ran away to get away from him."

"How do you know this?"

"Well, because she's a minor, the case was sealed. It just so happens that this investigator was able to get her hands on the original recording...through his ex-wife. It wasn't pretty. She let me listen to it and my stomach sank to the ground. Apparently her daughter was smart–she recorded the conversation using her boyfriend's phone. Not only did she record the conversation that she had with Tony earlier that week, she also recorded the conversation in which she was telling her mom what happened. And in the conversation with Tony, he apologized to her, saying that he would never do it again."

Shannon was silent.

"There's more. I went to lunch with his ex-wife–I flew to Indiana to meet with her. Turns out that Tony was gaslighting her and making her believe that she was bipolar. She's actually a very nice person. The part about her being an alcoholic is true–but she's been in AA ever since she got out of the hospital. Tony also had an affair while they were married."

"Wow. I don't even know what to say. This–this is a lot to take in."

"Look, I know you're engaged to him."

"How do you know that?" Shannon said in surprise.

"Jasper and her husband were out to dinner and they saw Tony propose to you. She told the rest of us. Because I was deep into investigating Tony, I made them all promise to stay quiet with you. I know you're hating me right now, but I just wanted to protect you until I had enough information about Tony to sit down with you. And there's more..."

"What more?"

"He really did attempt to murder his wife."

Shannon gasped.

"Tony was seeing another woman and his wife found out. She threatened to leave him and take the kids. Tony was afraid because she was drinking heavily at that time. She wasn't really in a position to take care of the kids–that part is true. So that night, he pretended to be interested in reviving their marriage and sweet-talked her. That night, they drank a lot of wine, but she noticed he wasn't getting drunk like she was. They were on their way upstairs to supposedly make love–she was following him up–and her daughter called at that moment. Her daughter had run away that very night and she told her mom that Tony forced himself on her the week before. So Denise was standing near the top of the stairs at that point and Tony overheard the conversation. He turned and pushed her down backwards, making it look like she just fell down the stairs after becoming dizzy. In court, it was her word against his. She had a very high level of alcohol in her blood along with her meds for bipolar–but because she was in a coma for two months and woke up with memory issues, the court dismissed the charges for the attempted murder and focused on what he did to his step-daughter."

"Holy shit. I'm just sitting here trying to make sense of all this. It just goes against everything I've been experiencing with Tony all this time."

"Shannon, you're in too deep with this, it's hard for you to be objective and see the reality. When I see Tony, I just remember the playboy in high school. I know you two had a friendship that ran deep back then, but now, I think he's playing you. You're his ticket to a new life. And...there's one more thing... remember my assistant, Ben?"

"Yeah."

"I sent him to that restaurant where Tony works–at that time I didn't know he worked there. Ben knew about Tony because I vented to him all the time and he became my sounding board when I first started working with the investigator. Well, Ben came back with our lunch order and told me he thought he saw Tony at the restaurant. Ben stepped out to have a smoke and saw Tony kissing one of the waitresses outside the side of the restaurant. It was quick and they went back in. Ben wasn't even sure it was Tony. So I sent the investigator over there a few times and she recorded them kissing."

Shannon started crying. "Oh my gosh, how could I have been so stupid? I'm on my way to Cabo. I have a wedding dress packed. We were going to get married and not tell anyone. We planned to have an actual wedding with all of you and the kids–when the time was right." The sobs came harder. Other passengers were looking at Shannon with sympathetic, curious eyes.

"What are you going to do?"

"I, I don't know."

"What the hell, Shannon! You can't be thinking of getting married to him!"

"I, I need time to process all of this, Marie. You dumped a tsunami on me. I feel like the Tony I know is nothing like the Tony you're telling me about. I've been happy with him. We are in love. I'm just sitting here, completely confused. I have to hear the recordings myself. I just can't wrap my mind around all this at once. I'm going to hang up here and give myself time to think and take all of this in."

"Please don't get on that plane. Please. You're gonna make a huge mistake. Come home. Don't do anything rash right now."

"I won't. I'll call you later."

Shannon sank back and put the phone down. Mascara was running down her face.

Wait, what if his ex-wife is lying?

But...there's the evidence from his daughter–the phone call that was recorded.

Oh my gosh, I love him. What am I going to do? How do I trust him? Wait, I can't trust him–he's already fooling around with a waitress at work!

Shannon took out a tissue and wiped the tears that were still streaming down her face.

"Are you okay?" The plump, matronly woman handed her more tissues.

"Not really, but thank you."

Just then, a text popped up.

Hey Red, I know you're probably boarding soon! Everything is all set here. The weather is absolutely perfect. It will be 75 and sunny tomorrow! Wait til you see the white roses and lilies! I met with the local preacher and he will join us over at Lover's Beach just before sunset. I arranged for a boat to take us over there. Don't forget your vows! I've got mine ready and I can't wait to share them with you. I can't wait until you walk off that plane and walk into my heart forever. I've got a couple of surprises for you. I'm so excited about our wedding—and our life together. See you at the airport soon! Text me when you take off. I love you, Shannon.

Shannon closed her eyes.

"Ladies and gentlemen, final boarding for Cabo San Lucas at gate B12. Just two minutes left to board. Please proceed to the gate quickly. The gate will be closing soon."

EPILOGUE

The bride and groom kissed.

Shannon watched as Zach's eyes filled with love. He bent over to kiss his new wife. They were young and in love. Fresh out of college with new jobs. Zach was an environmental engineer with a cushy office in downtown Austin. Susan was studying to become a veterinarian and worked as a manager at the local animal shelter. The two of them met at a college event and dated for two years.

Shannon looked over at Gary. He had his arm around his latest girlfriend and they seemed happy. The two of them exited the pew and followed the bride and groom down the aisle.

"Hey hon, should we go?"

Shannon smiled at her husband. "Yes, let's go." She took his arm. They walked down the aisle behind her ex-husband.

Marie caught up to them in the back of the church. "That was such a beautiful wedding! I'm glad I wore waterproof mascara. I was wiping my eyes every two seconds. Zach and Susan make such a beautiful couple. And Dr. Bob, I think I caught you blinking back a few!'

"Yeah, but at least I didn't cry as much as when Shannon and I got married!"

"For a neurosurgeon, you sure are a softie!" Marie gave him a playful punch on the arm.

"Hey, don't hurt me, I need that arm to operate," he laughed.

As they walked to the reception area, Shannon reflected on the years that passed. She thought back to the day she sat at the airport, watching the gate to Cabo close. Shannon immediately blocked Tony from her phone. She sat there motionless for a long while.

Shannon, please tell me you're okay!

Marie kept frantically texting, but Shannon didn't have the heart to respond. With a long sigh, she finally picked up the phone and dialed.

"It's about time, I was so worried about you! You're still at the airport?"

"Yeah."

"I'm so sorry, Shannon. I know this absolutely sucks right now, but you did the right thing. Marrying him would have been a huge mistake."

"I don't even know how to deal with what I'm feeling right now."

"I don't either. I hate seeing you hurt by all this. He's a damn jerk for what he put you through."

"Look, I can't talk anymore. I gotta figure out how to get home. I'll talk to you later after I get home."

The next flight home was leaving in 45 minutes and she had to run to purchase a ticket and get on the flight. Shannon went home and told the boys the whole sordid story. She had them block Tony from their phone.

The next day, Shannon called Tony's ex-wife. At first, the woman was hesitant to share any details, but they ended up talking for three hours. Little by little, Denise told Shannon about her life with Tony. She played the incriminating recording between Tony and her daughter. Shannon couldn't bear to finish listening to it–within the first minute or two, she had heard enough. She couldn't even listen to the entire recording between Denise and her daughter– the pain in their voices was just too much. Denise gave Shannon her daughter's phone number and another long conversation ensued.

Shannon wrote Tony a long letter outlining all the things that Marie had found out as well as her conversations with his ex-wife and step-daughter. Shannon sent the letter to the restaurant by certified mail. Tony sent her a letter back, but Shannon immediately went to the garbage and ripped it up. Nothing he could ever write would justify the deception he dragged her through.

One evening, the doorbell rang, and Shannon peered through the window. Tony was standing at the front door, holding a bouquet of white roses and lilies. She quietly receded to the bedroom. There was no way she was ever going to speak to him again. Tony tried twice more to show up on her doorstep and each time, she refused to answer the door.

Shannon sent another certified letter to the restaurant, this time written by her lawyer asking him to cease and desist any contact with her.

After a couple of months of therapy, Shannon finally felt a glimmer of joy. She decided to compete again and made some new friends at the rodeos. Her mare, Soul Girl, was a seasoned pro and they moved around the barrels like poetry together.

The first day that Shannon met Dr. Bob was by accident, literally. She was rounding a corner holding apple juice and graham crackers for a mom who just gave birth at three a.m. She collided right into Dr. Bob, the new neurosurgeon.

"I'm so sorry! I didn't see you."

Dr. Bob picked up the apple juice and gave it back to Shannon. "Good thing those things are sealed well. I'm Dr. Bob. Neurosurgeon. I like to open people's brains and play around with them," he grinned.

"Shannon, head nurse, Labor and Delivery. I

occasionally catch babies when the doctors and midwives don't show up in time. What brings you to our department?"

"Ah, my niece just had her first baby and I thought I would stop by to see her. She just popped her son out about an hour ago. Room 321."

"I'm on my way over there now. Beautiful baby!"

By the end of the shift, Dr. Bob asked Shannon to grab breakfast with him in the cafeteria.

Three years later, they got married.

ABOUT THE AUTHOR

Anne Valle

Anne grew up thinking she would be a famous author, but didn't write her first novel until she was 58. You're holding this first novel in your hands, (or your phone, or your computer/laptop.)

Anne spends most of her time writing stories, walking in the woods, or on the water somewhere. Occasionally she cooks and feeds her family and friends. Mostly she loves to explore new restaurants and have someone else hand over the food.

Speaking of family, a big thank you goes out to Ren, Anne's brilliant daughter, who also happens to be her editor. Anne extends a big thank you to the early readers who willingly gave up a few hours to point out typos and other errors.

Another big thank you goes to her launch team, who rallied together to help spread the word about this book. They all gave a thumbs up to this book–so Anne hopes that you do, too. Leave a sparkling review, talk about the book, and share it with your friends so that Anne can continue to write more entertaining novels. And thank YOU for being a part of this!